praise

"It is fairly easy to describe domestic desperation—not so easy to make the spectacle a work of art. Author Keith Banner delivers characters of the new working class in Cincinnati, Indiana, Dayton… Banner shows you people who are squeezed on all sides—and makes you glad you saw."

—*Cincinnati Magazine*

"Keith Banner's new collection stands next to nothing, but all by itself, distinguished by a hard-won realism of the modern working class, amid the abandoned malls and the barely surviving towns of the rustbelt. This is Raymond Carver reinvented, filtered through a dark and richly queer perspective."

—CHRISTOPHER BARZAK, author of *One for Sorrow*

"Keith Banner's stories are point-blank realistic. Working-class lives peppered with the detritus of pop culture and the small movie-real moments that even the most unremarkable lives contain. They're beautiful, but they'll bum you out, but you'll love them anyway." —L.A. FIELDS, author of *My Dear Watson*

NEXT TO NOTHING

Next to Nothing

stories

Keith Banner

Lethe Press
Maple Shade, New Jersey

Next to Nothing: Stories

Published in 2014 by Lethe Press, Inc.
118 Heritage Avenue • Maple Shade, NJ 08052-3018 USA
www.lethepressbooks.com • lethepress@aol.com
ISBN: 978-1-59021-177-9 / 1-59021-177-4
e-ISBN: 978-1-59021-178-6 / 1-59021-178-2

Some of these stories were previously published: "Winners Never Sleep!" first
appeared in the anthology *Keeping the Wolves at Bay: Emerging Writers*; "Next to
Nothing" on the website *Lodestar Quarterly*; "From Me to You" in *Third Coast*;
"Queers Can't Hear" on *Black & Grey*; "Lowest of the Low" on *The Still Blue Project*;
"How to Get from This to This" in the anthology *Everything I Have Is Blue*; and
"Princess Is Sleeping" in *Other Voices*.

These stories are works of fiction. Names, characters, places, and incidents either
are the products of the author's imagination or are used fictitiously, and any
resemblance to actual persons, living or dead, business establishments, events, or
locales is entirely coincidental.

Set in Minion and Gill Sans.
Cover and interior design: Alex Jeffers.
Cover images: Carl Ballou (front); Piotr Machalski (back).

LIBRARY OF CONGRESS CATALOGING-IN-PUBLICATION DATA
Banner, Keith.
   [Short stories. Selections]
   Next to nothing : stories / Keith Banner.
      pages cm
   ISBN 978-1-59021-177-9 (Paperback : alk. paper)
   I. Title.
   PS3552.A4948A6 2014
   813'.54--dc23
                        2013044231

Thanks: Steve Berman, Robbin Brown, Andrew Cole, Cathy Dailey, Sharon Dilworth, LA Fields, Nathanial Jacks, Matt Morris, Donald Ray Pollock, MR Purdue, Wendell Ricketts, Terri Schelter-Chenault, Krystn Shopp, Melissa Williams, and especially Bill Ross.

Table of Contents

"It is when the freak can be sensed as a figure for our essential displacement that he attains some depth in literature."

—Flannery O'Connor, *Mystery and Manners*

Winners Never Sleep!

I

I manage the laundromat Leslie owns. Six months ago we went out to eat at Steak N Shake to celebrate my five-year anniversary there.

"I've never trusted an employee like I trust you, Rodney," Leslie said.

His old face, like ET's, made me feel sad and grateful. He used to be a projectionist at a movie theater downtown before it closed. After his wife died, he spent what money they had saved to buy the laundromat. Every once in a while I wonder what he would think if he'd seen me when I used to do drag. Gold and orange outfits, face made up like a beautiful whore's, lips as glossy-red as spit-out cinnamon candy. Back then I was skinny as hell. He would probably just get a kick out of it and smile. He might say, "Shady past, eh?" Something like that.

The gift Leslie presented to me at the Steak N Shake was health insurance.

"Now," he said. "You go see about that stomach stapling thing you told me about." He took a big gulp of his coffee and looked me in the eye and winked.

"I wish my wife had gotten that surgery," Leslie said. His wife had been extremely overweight like yours truly (I am now at three hundred and ninety-six pounds). She died of a stroke when she was forty-nine. No kids or anything. Leslie is always sympathizing.

"Thank you," I said.

"Why, you are very welcome, sir."

He looked around the restaurant for the waitress.

"Don't you even think about paying," he said.

2

Ten years ago I had a boyfriend named James Partlow. He had a goatee, a sun-tan-booth complexion and beautiful, glazed-over eyes. I met him while doing his mother's hair in my apartment (my beautician's license had expired). Irena was her name. We always had a good time—two bitches bitching it up, one with renegade hairstyling skills, the other one skinny from alcoholism and loneliness, wanting to look like Sharon Stone.

I was in shorts and a tank top and flip-flops, not made up at all, just leisurely male-stylish. Irena was on a kitchen chair, hair wet, severe chin tucked down into a pink towel. I'd popped in a Mel Gibson movie, the one where he was bestial and blue-faced in a kilt. That was what Irena wanted. No sound from the TV, just Janet Jackson's greatest hits coming out of my kitchen boombox.

"I had to fire my district manager," Irena said as I snipped.

"He stealing from you?"

"Yup."

"Shit," I whispered, cutting away.

It was summer. My windows were open to the big city of Dayton, Ohio, where I had a lovely downtown apartment near a little row of restaurants and bars. Suddenly there he was, standing right outside my screen door: goatee, camouflage shorts, Birkenstock clogs, a Bob Marley tee-shirt. His hair was pitch black and shaved, except for the top, which was a little wild and gelled to stay that way.

He knocked and I was thinking he was here for a drug deal I'd forgotten about.

"Come on in, James," Irena said.

"That's your little boy?"

Irena laughed. "He's my little baby."

He walked in and told his mom to shut up and she barked back a big laugh.

"He's my chauffeur today because my BMW is getting some detail work."

James looked at me. Automatically I flashed on the relationship between the drummer in Culture Club and Boy George.

He sat down and said, "What in the fuck is on the TV?"

"*Braveheart*," Irena said.

I plugged in the blow-dryer.

"I hate this fucking movie!" James said really loud above the blow-dryer sound.

I smiled at him and he smiled back at me. It was the eyes that got me, glassy and sensitive and full of little tricks to play on people who didn't understand his predicament being a momma's-boy-slash-chauffeur-slash-fag-slash-whatever-else-he-decided-he-was-at-that-moment.

I finished, gave Irena an ornate handheld mirror.

"You never disappoint, Rodney." She looked over at James with a smart-ass glare. Janet was singing "The Pleasure Principle."

"Thank you, sweetie," I said. "Do you want another drink? James, would you like anything?"

"No thanks." Suddenly he was standing right near me, smelling of CK-One.

"He's trying to quit drinking," Irena whispered, standing up. She was way taller than he was.

James grinned. Irena, in a lavender summery pantsuit, ripped the check she'd just written out.

"Rodney is a female impersonator," she said. "Look at the pictures, James."

Professional and Polaroid, in frames, they were all over the walls. I thought of my apartment as my office. When club owners came over for drugging and drinking, I would do a little impromptu "thing" for them so I might be able to headline gigs, or emcee shows, have my pick.

"Pretty," he said, pointing at me in Chicago, doing "I Touch Myself" by the Divinyls in black vinyl and mesh-net and hair like a blonde Elvira.

"Just plain pretty," he said. His voice was a practiced growl and whisper. It sounded like a cross between Jesus Christ and personal-trainer-with-a-drug-problem.

"Let's go, James," Irena said, getting her purse. "You like?" she said to him about her hair.

"Rodney, you're great. She looks one-*thousand*-percent better."

Irena playfully slapped at James.

Once they were gone, I saw he had left his business card on my coffee table. It was mint-green and featured a frog in top-hat and tails: JAMES PARTLOW, CONSULTANT.

The next day I called him and it was like we had known each other for years. I invited him to my weekend show at Petting Zoo, this little club. He said he would be honored.

After my show, I went out to the bar floor still in drag. I was in an emerald-green cocktail dress, slit to the hipbone, blonde wig puffed out like a contemporary and sweetly fiendish Dale Evans, black heels, black hose. James was at a table by himself. I sat down. The place wasn't packed, just slightly crowded. I knew everybody.

"You were fantastic," he said.

Drinks came and then more drinks. Drinks, drinks, drinks.

"I mean, come on, I just loved it," he said. More and more compliments. "If you can't tell, I was mighty impressed."

I kept smiling. He leaned in close, whispering above the music.

"It is the biggest fucking turn-on," he said. Then he came over to me and kissed me on the mouth.

That first night he just wouldn't stop. It was at my place, all-out stupefying lust. The next morning he went and got breakfast for us at one of the three McDonald's location his mom owned. Pancakes, sausage, eggs, coffee, all in Styrofoam. We ate at my dinette set.

"Man," he said, sipping from the cup. "I was so turned on."

"Me too."

"You performing tonight too?"

"Yeah, same place." I delicately shoveled in little bitty bites of scrambled egg, tenderly chewing and swallowing microscopic portions, eyes dewy.

"I'm there," he said and laughed.

I took all of it in like I deserved it.

+

Three months later, James moved in. I found out his consulting business was basically his mom paying him to do whatever she told him to do. When she fired the district manager, James had to do some district-managing until he found a replacement. When Irena had her bathroom redone, he had to sit in the house waiting for the plumber while she went to New Mexico for a few days with lady friends.

For a while it was kind of special to be caught up in his Momma's Boy Paradise: him scolding Irena for her alcoholism and cleaning up the puke in her mansion in the suburbs of Dayton, then coming to my show and getting drunk and fucking me afterwards.

The closer we got to the Las Vegas incident, though, the more I was feeling like the movie we were making was taking a turn toward inevitable conflict.

He told me he did not want me doing his mom's hair anymore.

"You'll just talk about me. Or she will," he said.

"Does she know?" I asked.

"What?"

"That we're an item?" I was making microwavable popcorn on a Tuesday night. We'd rented movies.

"No."

I laughed, pressing the buttons.

"Does she even know you're a fag, honey?"

"Yeah," he said and laughed. "She knows that."

But then he got very quiet.

We watched the movies and ate the popcorn and got drunk on whatever I had. I went into my bedroom around 11:30 and put on my face so he could be turned on. I came out naked, in a wig, face all dolled up. We did it in the living room for a while, then took it to the bedroom, and the next day he left without telling me. No note, nothing. He came back around 3:00. I had a client, this sweet elderly lady with the wispiest hair, like cobwebs. I was struggling with what I had to do. There he was, knocking on the screen door.

"Come on in," I said.

He shook his head no. The elderly lady was half-asleep but I went out on the porch. He was afraid maybe she might know his mom.

"Mom's in rehab. I just took her." He was grinning like George Michael during the Wham! years.

"Shit. She okay?"

"Yeah, she's fine—she'll dry out and pretend she's okay and come back. But here's the sweet part. She and a friend of hers were supposed to go to to Vegas tomorrow for three days. Irrevocable tickets, baby. Her friend doesn't want to go now, so it's me and you. Vegas!"

He held me and jumped up and down, then stopped.

"Pack your bags. I'll be back around 6:00."

He sped off in his shiny Miata. I went back in and the elderly lady in the beige outfit, with that brittle hair, was smiling almost wickedly.

"Someone has a beau," she said, winking.

+

I packed some clothes, thinking three days in Vegas would mean jeans and tee-shirts, maybe a suit and shoes. Finally around 8:30, James showed up with his eyes bugging out. He told me he was taking a lot of speed because Vegas was the city that never sleeps.

"That's New York," I said.

He laughed real loud. I didn't say anything else.

"You ready, baby? We have to be at the airport by 11:00." He looked like a momma's boy with a deep dark secret. "You got any stuff?"

We did a few lines together. When he came up for air, he went over to the two suitcases I had packed, opened one up, looked in.

Said: "No, no, no. *No!*"

"What?" I got up from the couch, taking the mirror to the kitchen sink, rinsing it off.

He took one of the suitcases into the bedroom and dumped the clothes out, laughing.

"This is our vacation!" He was yelling.

"What?" I had a high pitch to my voice now, feeling dazed, my head a helicopter piloted by the Tiny Powerful Princess of Cocaine Island.

"I want you to be my baby the whole time," he said in the bedroom, opening my closet. He took out some shoes and gowns, threw them onto the bed, next to the clothes he dumped out.

"Wait a fucking minute," I said.

I never did drag to pass in broad daylight. I never wanted to be a real lady-lady: have my dick cut off, get real tits, shots and all that. I've had friends who did that, sure, but that was not in *my* program, okay? It was always about being Me and living it up, pancaked and pretty in that sick big way, someone to be feared if you really got down to the nitty-gritty. At times it felt like the only power I had was up on the nightclub stage, costumed and lip-syncing, at the center of my own marvelous little universe.

"I don't do it unless I'm on stage, James," I said. "Or here, you know, with you."

"Come on. For me. We'll be other people. I'm gonna wear my sunglasses the whole time. We'll call each other different names, huh? I'll be, um, David St. Thomas. You pick a name."

He was panting a little. He came over and whispered, "Pick a name," and his hot breath slid into my ear canal like a finger. I thought about saying no again. But I got my other suitcase out of the living room instead. I unpacked it, threw in some of my outfits, shoes and make-up in Ziploc bags. He clapped his hands.

"We are gonna have fun every motherfucking night!" he said.

I think that was from a Prince song.

+

Glassy heat like light bulbs melting confronted me as soon as we got out of the Vegas airport. I wasn't in drag on the plane. He gave me that at least. We jumped in a cab and James told the cabby, "The Aladdin, please."

The cab smelled of cigars and pee and old-man. Outside the back windows, the mid-morning sun glittered at its meanest. Down the strip, all the neon looked ghostly from being outshined. I wanted a drink suddenly, something precious, a Cosmopolitan or Cape Cod.

Brilliant acid-blue sky turned into dark musty plush inside Aladdin's. Huge ornate statues of Aladdin's lamp and magic carpets were painted on the ceiling. James registered us in at the front desk, got us to the room, gave me my own card-key. The room was cool and smoke-free but I lit up. I spread the curtains to see that radioactive sunshine, the tops of awnings, Caesar's Palace catty-corner, a big billboard with Robin Williams on it.

James downed a glass of water.

"Get ready," he said, sitting on the edge of the bed, waiting for his pills to start.

Once my whole cosmetics laboratory was set up on the big marble sink, I got out of my man clothes and started doing my face. James shut the curtains, crashed on the bed, then got back up and turned on the TV. He kept scratching at his eyebrows. It took me an hour of fussing. I had one wig for two days. It was blonde and not too showy, Meg Ryan-ish, perky-fluffy.

When I was through, you still knew it was me, of course. James was behind me, sun-glasses and leather sport coat, hair freshly moussed. That tanning-booth tan.

"You look great, hon."

I stood up and pressed out my mint-green skirt. I looked down at my black high heels and hose. For a second I felt the thrill of being someone else entirely, not a drag queen but a stylish lady in Las Vegas, in complete control of her life and her pleasures. I felt pulled together to the point that I thought yes this might work. But then James kissed me like he had never kissed me before—a mother kiss, a fake kiss—and I knew I had fallen into a trap.

Down the elevator. On one floor, a fat old man in a Hawaiian shirt and dress pants and Italian loafers looked away from me, then back, without a smile or indication of a smile, like he knew what I was trying to do here and it was just not worth going into. James and I walked out into the casino proper. James automatically sat down at a slot machine, slid fifty bucks in, and pulled the lever down.

"Sit next to me," he whispered. "Be my lucky charm. By the way, what's your name?"

He bummed a cigarette from me, and I lit it for him after I sat down. Even though there was major A-C blowing, there was still a smell of awful gar-bagey heat and other people's cigarette coughs. I lit up, our knees touched, and he kept pulling down the lever: nothing. He told me to get closer. I told him my new name.

"Ruth." Which was my mother's name.

"Ruth?" He laughed. "That's fucking depressing. That's fucking Biblical."

He pulled the lever and yet again nothing. I told him I had to pee, and he whispered, "Don't forget to use the *ladies'* room, Ruthie."

I felt shaky when I saw myself bathed in fluorescence in the lady's room mirror. Women left and came in, a giggle here a giggle there. I looked like a fucked-up drag queen with jet lag, about as real as Ronald McDonald. Rhonda McDonald, his desperate drag-queen brother.

After I used the bathroom, I returned to the casino, telling myself that I was going to get through *just tonight* like this. Then tomorrow it was back into jeans and a nice shirt and James and I would laugh about this. I went to the slot machine he'd been at. Its screen belched out lights and honks.

But James was gone.

I looked everywhere: by the huge spiral staircase, the three or four fancy bars that lined the way to a mall with a ceiling painted like sky. During my search I completely lost the ability to pretend I was Meg Ryan. I even went outside to look for James, and the heat started to melt my make-up. I went back into the casino, to the slot machines, blackjack and roulette tables. Nothing. No sign of James.

I sat down by the front entrance and waited. Went for a walk and waited again. Put some quarters into a slot machine. But still I felt like I was slipping into a hole I never even knew was there. Being in Vegas, this drippy, lost Meg Ryan wannabe, I had the urge to scream and rip at my clothes and hit myself. All I really wanted was simple: for James to come to me and apologize and tell me he loved me, you know, like in a Meg Ryan movie. This was all I wanted in the whole wide world that moment.

I walked around some more. I knew I could just go upstairs and take everything off but somehow I wasn't able. I wound up outside a smorgasbord called the Spice Market Buffet, on the other side of the casino. A big bulletin board displayed exotic culinary delights, like Indian and Thai fare, glistening in beautiful backlit photographs.

I realized I was starving.

The buffet was down a small escalator. The host seated me all alone near a mirrored wall in an orange velour booth. The carpet was maroon wall to wall. All the smells of food merged into one, a creamy, oniony vapor. I grabbed myself a plate, dressed up like I was, and went to each little island of food, taking as much as I wanted.

I knew even then what this was: finding out how to survive by putting everything into my mouth. Spaghetti and shrimp and pesto and apple pie, Bananas Foster and tacos and olives and pickles and crepes. As I ate, I remembered the feeling of putting on a dress when I was nine, the secrecy and the pleasure and the custom-made power, like I was shifting the way the world went just by doing one little goddamn personal thing.

And I realized I had stumbled onto a new way to make myself into something else.

Soon as I finished (I was there for a very long time), I got up, dizzy with all I had consumed, filled up to the top of my skull with sumptuousness. After taking care of the bill, I went back to the room.

James came in toward dawn, saying, "Where the hell did you disappear to?"

He was red-faced and fucked-up, smelling of cigarettes and booze and sex, wearing a tee-shirt that said "Winners Never Sleep!"

When he got into the bed, I could not move. He kissed my cheek.

"You mad at me?" he said.

I didn't answer. I couldn't even ask him where he had disappeared to. It didn't matter anymore. I looked at his face in the TV-lit dark. The sunglasses were off, but his eyes still looked hidden. I felt like a cornucopia had been shoved into my mouth. I had a new way of life. The next morning there would be breakfast and there would be lunch after that. And dinner. And dessert. And a midnight snack.

"Should you sleep with all that shit on your face?" he whispered.

Then he just conked out.

+

We woke up the next day and I told him I wasn't a lady any more. He got totally pissed. We basically wound up having separate vacations.

His mom committed accidental suicide a few months later (pills and vodka). I was going to go to her funeral, but it just didn't seem wise. Now I think James owns a car lot in Indiana somewhere.

After that trip, as I gained more weight, I began to lose what I had been. I bought new drag outfits to suit my new physique, making sure everyone I performed in front of understood that I got the joke.

"Look here at this motherfucking heifer," I'd say in between lip-syncing songs, but then even the fun of that evaporated.

I was just the fat-ass drag queen pretending to be a drag queen, which I understood, but the show offers got fewer and further between, and the men did too. One day I took everything out to the dumpster, shoes and gowns and wigs and all those pictures on the walls, just like that. It was October, almost dusk. I got into my car after I threw everything away and drove to a Kentucky Fried Chicken drive-through. I took a whole bucket of chicken, mashed potatoes and gravy, three little chocolate brownie desserts, and a two-liter of Pepsi back to my apartment and ate it all in two hours. At the end of this feast, almost breathless from stuffing myself, I contemplated what I had become. The answer was simple. I got this way by humiliating myself in a mint-green skirt outfit in Las Vegas for some idiot in sunglasses who needed me to do that so he could be what he was.

Sadly nobody was really stirred up enough to pull me from my downward spiral. Even the old ladies who once wanted me to be their own personal stylist, even they kind of picked up on the smell. I wanted out, and I was getting exactly what I wanted. They just wanted to have their hair done.

3

Leslie picks me up at 6:00 in the morning the day of my stomach bypass.

I use my cane to get to his car, and he is smiling.

"Morning, kiddo."

"Thanks Leslie," I say. I have a little suitcase.

It's muggy. He has a large Lincoln Continental with the A-C turned up high, light rock on the radio. Every once in a while, in his sad-old-man voice, Leslie talks about the weather we're having, and how I am not to worry about my recovery and coming back to my job. I smile. I feel like I am being taken to a concentration camp.

"This is gonna change your life, my friend," he tells me, parking in the garage.

"You don't have to go in."

"I don't mind. I'll go in until you get situated."

We both walk through the almost empty garage, through a corridor of yellow walls, to the reception desk at the Weight Clinic. The office is light blue with off-white chairs and gray wall-to-wall. I've been here many times, for check-ups and tests and talks. It took five months of waiting for the insurance to okay my surgery and for the preliminary tests to come through. But here it is, the day I am to be transformed, at least internally.

I look over at Leslie: white dress-shirt, sleeves with red rubber bands to keep them rolled up, those glasses, gray-green pants, sneakers. He has on a dark brown fedora as well. I want to know why Leslie is being so kind but I just don't have the courage to ask him.

I think: what if ten years ago on the plane to Vegas the stewardess had offered me a crystal ball instead of a bag of peanuts? I would have looked into it and seen this scene, not really knowing I was in it, and definitely not knowing who the hell the little Jiminy Cricket man was. I would have shaken the damn crystal ball hard and looked again and would have seen the same scene and told the flight attendant, "Ma'am, there is definitely something wrong with this thing."

It's almost like Leslie is the gift you get when you give up on people. You get this unassuming, almost invisible man who owns the laundromat where you spend your days washing other people's clothes and giving people the key to the bathroom. Leslie is the one to escort you to your next place. Of course I wonder what James is doing right at this moment.

I fill out more papers. Then we're waiting. One other morbidly obese person, who's with her thin mother, is doing the same thing I am: sitting, waiting. In little glimpses, I look at her brown hair tied back into a ponytail, her pale jowls, her sweet empty eyes.

"This is a nice place," Leslie whispers. He smiles with yellow teeth, two or three silver ones.

They don't really cut you all the way open. It's a laser-beam, a tiny fierce finger that slices through what you have done to yourself. I can feel the singe already, searing through flab and feelings, satisfying my need to be something else. But that need gets smaller and smaller as I wait, until finally it vanishes completely. All that's left is pure fear, which is somehow a comfort to me.

I get up.

I walk out as fast as I can with my cane. Once I get back to the yellow corridor, Leslie catches up. He has the suitcase I left behind.

"They're calling for you," Leslie is saying. He's confused, but he's smiling.

I lean up against the wall.

"I can't do it," I whisper.

"What?" Leslie says.

"I can't do it."

We just stand there in the corridor. Leslie whispers a few things, but I tell him again that I can't do it. I don't want to know what else might happen.

"Take me home," I say. "I just want to go home."

+

Leslie and I spend the rest of the day together. He rents some movies. I have brownie mix and have enough energy to make brownies. It starts to rain. Leslie has the good sense not to be angered by my cowardice. Maybe he thinks I'll eventually go through with the surgery, maybe he thinks I really know what's best.

"I like the old ones," he says, shoving one of his selections from Blockbuster into the DVD player. There's the softest thunder. I'm on the couch. The brownies are cooling. I am watching the TV screen, then I look at Leslie's face.

"Can I get you anything else?" he says.

Next to Nothing

Tuesday morning, I'm out front of the Ponderosa Steakhouse, changing the sign. It's hotter than hell. I'm wearing my clip-on necktie, short-sleeved shirt, brown pants. Tall, lanky and going bald, I use a long pole with a suction cup on it to get the letters up. But they keep dropping like dead birds. I have a tattoo on my upper left arm. Guess what it says? "Never surrender."

I'm spelling: 8/30 IS OUR LAST DAY OF BUSINESS. THANKS FOR YOUR PA-TRONAGE.

I'm not even sad about us closing down. I don't get sad. Every evening, I take four Tylenol PMs, conk out, wake up to three or four cups of black coffee. I have some caffeine gum on hand at all times. There's a prescription antidepressant I take off and on.

My brother-in-law's inside the restaurant, pulling stuff off the back shelves: cans of corn and soup and baked apples that used to go onto the salad bar. I pulled some strings and got him hired to relocate stock to the Pondo that's still open in Dayton. He got laid off last week.

Ron is scrawny but has big arms and the dumbest, prettiest eyes, and a thin-lipped mouth with a mustache you want to wipe off with a paper towel. My sister married him in 1991, and they have two kids, the nephews I try to avoid. One of the nephews is slow and likes to start fires. The other one is good at science and computers.

I happen to be a little sweet on Ron. Sounds pretty messed up, but that's me. Actually, I've been falling for him since I had cancer two years back and had to move in with my sister's family to be taken care of. Lung cancer. (Yes, I still smoke.) My sister was standoffish throughout that whole ordeal, like she wished I would just go off somewhere and die. But Ron treated me like some long-lost pal he wanted to make sure he saved. I'd get home from chemo and, since he was working nights, he'd be up and he'd roll me some weed and we'd get high in the basement, talking about Led Zeppelin or Cheech and Chong or *Friday the 13th*. You know, our childhoods.

Right now, sweat-soaked and shaky, I'm concentrating so hard that the words I do manage to get up there on the sign don't make sense anymore. But in forty-five minutes I have completed my task. I walk into the Pondo's backdoor holding the suction-cup pole and the milk-crate of leftover red plastic letters. Ron comes out with a cardboard box of canned baked beans.

"I've got one side out. I'm running it over right now." He smiles at me. I smile back and throw the pole and letters into the back room, grab a roll of paper towels to sop up my sweaty forehead. My cell phone goes off, but it's just a hang-up. I go back outside.

"You're good at moving stuff," I say.

He's pushing that box of beans into his big rusty Ford truck, the one his dad gave him.

"Yeah," he says. I hear a sort of pride in his voice that would probably make my sister pissed at him. They just separated last week.

"Hey," he says, and I walk closer to him. He lights a cigarette. I light one up too. "How's that dog?"

"I'm afraid I'm gonna have to get rid of him soon. I swear to God."

Ron laughs. "I'm sorry but maybe you should have seen that one coming, buddy."

"I know, I know." I laugh too.

It is pretty funny. About six months back I adopted a greyhound after hearing about this SAVE THE GREYHOUNDS campaign on the news. These evildoers were raising the dogs to race at a track over in Indiana, but as soon as they couldn't race anymore they were killed. I saw that on TV and I just burst into tears. Glassy-eyed greyhounds were in cages waiting to be shot up with lethal injections. I mean, come on.

So I called the agency that does the saving of the dogs and they hooked me up with Sebastian (that's what I named him, and I still don't know why). He didn't look so big out in the muddy field where I got him, behind the pound, but he did look kind of odd: bicycle-seat-shaped head and devilish eyes and curved-in body. I remember putting him into my car, in the backseat, how he just seemed to love being in a car. He didn't bark once, until we got to my apartment.

"I was hoping Janet might take him. Someone to replace you," I say. The smoke goes into my lungs like a plug into a socket.

Ron laughs at my little joke. We're always joking.

"Yeah. That's all I ever was to her—some stupid runt dog. We'll get back together though. I'm pretty sure. She's just in one of her moods."

True—she's always kicking him out. But this time it seems more permanent. Like tomorrow she and the nephews are going on a vacation that was supposed to be for the whole family, Disney World and the whole works, with money from their income-tax check. But Ron lost his job at the warehouse and he started getting high again. No Disney World for him. *He could go to hell for his vacation*—that's Janet talking right there.

I put my cigarette out, look at Ron standing in the sunshine, with pit stains and a smile. Something pathetic in him speaks directly to the pathetic in me. He has the sense of optimism it takes to not have a job and yet be able to belly laugh at *Home Improvement* and eat a whole pizza and smoke dope and play on his sons' Xbox all day.

"I'm going over to the Dayton place and drop this off."

"Great."

"Hey," Ron says. "Give me a hug."

That's something Ron does. Hugs people.

When he does, he whispers right into my ear, "Thanks, buddy, for getting me this job."

He walks off like he's embarrassed. I go back into the Pondo. Part of the dining room is already closed off. The salad bar is completely shut down, like an abandoned yacht, with its scarred-up sneeze-shield and empty holes where the plastic containers for dressings used to slide in. Some of the décor has been taken off the walls. The owner is a big fat homo, Jack Stroganavski. We all call him Jack Stroganoff, sometimes Beef Stroganoff, sometimes just Beef or Stroke. He owns the Pondo in Dayton too.

The day Jack told me the place had finally and totally gone under, about two months back, I was closing, and he was, as usual, coming on to me in the meat locker. I was counting frozen T-bones and New York strips. He stood in the doorway, against the thick plastic flaps inside the door, in his Hawaiian shirt, khaki shorts and flip-flops. Jack thinks being rich means dressing like a drunk, obnoxious tourist.

"It's done. I gotta close this one. I mean, this place is bleeding money." He had a big frown on. "The goddamn Applebee's and TGI Friday's out by the bypass killed us."

"I know," I said, but I felt that sense of having everything pulled out from under me. I looked at the frozen T-bones in their box. I'm quite thorough when I'm doing inventory. I pull out every last piece of meat. Cannot stand coming up short.

Then Jack Stroganoff was right in my face in the freezer, big-bellied Jimmy Buffet wannabe who drives a Hummer.

"If you don't mind the drive, I can offer you management at the Dayton store." He licked his lips almost like a joke.

"I'll think about it."

But then he was crying. He was touching my face.

"Can you tell the employees for me?"

He kissed me. I realized he might be the loneliest person on earth. Then he tongued me and the whole thing had to stop. He laughed, walking backwards, wiping the tears from his face.

"You kill me," he said in his singsong way.

+

Sebastian may have swallowed my cell phone. I can't find it. He doesn't look like he feels good, big gray dog on a sad beige sofa. The apartment is the same as usual, total disarray, with the smell of dog. I dial my cell-phone number from my home phone and listen to Sebastian's stomach. Ron answers.

"Hello?"

"Ron?"

"Yeah, bud. You left your cell phone in the stock room. I came back after my last haul, and got it for you. It's on my way. I know you and your phone." He laughs.

"I thought I'd lost the thing again," I say, laughing too. The thought of him coming over makes me feel like life might sometimes be fair after all. "I was going into cell-phone withdrawal."

"Cool. I'm on my way. You want me to stop and get a pizza?"

"Sure."

My window-unit air-conditioner works wonders, nice chill. After I straighten up the place I sit back and drink some white wine with Soapnet on. It's about 8:00 PM. Earlier today, after work, I went and interviewed at Olive Garden. Not for management, for waiting tables. They offered me the position right then and there. I took it. No more responsibility, except for myself. No more counting meat. Just tips. We can celebrate that.

Sebastian comes over and tries to do his tiny-dog-curl-up thing on my lap, knocking the shade off a lamp in the process. I just let him have his way with me. I think about when I was sick, staying at my sister's house. She tried to ignore me even though she was driving me to and from chemo sessions. Having been dumped out in her driveway, I'd walk in and Ron would be there with the biggest doobie in Clermont County. This one time we got so high I didn't even puke once. Imagine me, with *all* my hair coming out, and him with his sweet, sleepy eyes, watching *Scream* DVDs: the Sick Fag and the Low-Achieving Husband.

"She thought you had AIDS. I think she still thinks that," Ron told me when he was putting in *Scream 2*.

"No. Not AIDS. Salems. I got a bad case of the Salems." (I mean, I did like four packs a day at one point.)

"She doesn't like you being so gay," Ron said. Then he laughed. "I don't give a shit, but she sure does."

"I think she's a closet dyke myself," I said.

"Don't think so," Ron said. "She loves sex. I'm not kidding. That gal could go all night." The grin he had on made it look like he was almost afraid of her.

"Enough," I said.

"She loves you though."

"You think?"

Ron came over and sat down next to me, his body closer than usual.

"I don't want you to die. She doesn't either. You're a good person. You have a good heart, Den."

Those four sentences took hold like little hands clawing into dirt, pulling me out of it. I didn't say anything. I didn't tell Ron that his kindness might have been the main reason I was staying alive. That, plus half a lung being removed, and the chemo and a few trips to radiation-land.

+

Soon as Ron shows up, Janet calls me on my cell phone. Ron hands it over to me.

"Why in the hell does Ron have your cell phone?"

"He found it at work… So what's up?"

"I really did not need to hear his voice," she says. I hear Brandon, the slow one, in the background. He's yelling something about wanting to eat where they have the *Tomb Raider 2* toy.

"I'm sorry. So what's up?"

"Does he talk about me?"

Ron opens the pizza box on the coffee-table. Some music video with Pink is on the TV. He just sits, and all he is thinking about is pizza and Pink and pot, you can tell. The three Ps.

"Sometimes."

"Look. Forget it. Doesn't matter. He's out. The reason I called you is I want you to house-sit for us. Tammy was gonna do it but she has some gallbladder thing—don't ask. You can house-sit, right?"

"Can I bring Sebastian?"

"Devil dog? I guess. But he has to stay outside."

"Sure."

"We're leaving tomorrow morning. You still got a key?"

"No."

"Well, we're leaving at 8:00, so come over about then and I'll give you the key. Love you." She says that last part like she's just gotten through a choking fit at a dinner table and has to apologize for it.

"Love you too."

She's gone. I go over and get a slice and sit down on a chair. Ron's got the remote. He's smoking a joint. He looks like a cross between Bambi and Burt Reynolds when he smokes weed.

"She ask about me?" he says.

"Yeah. She wanted to know if you were talking about her."

"What did you say?"

"Sometimes. Me and Sebastian are going to house-sit."

He looks hurt, like she should have asked him to house-sit.

"I miss her and the boys," Ron says, eyes closed.

"I bet."

He gets up and gives me the doobie. He shuts the TV off and starts looking through my CDs on the floor.

"I hate where I'm staying," he says. "Fucking roach motel."

Sebastian sits down on the couch with a loud sad yawn. His face looks worried, and he lets out a couple barks, and then closes his face down like a light bulb. I go down on the floor with the joint and give it back to Ron.

"You got any Fleetwood Mac?"

"Somewhere."

When I reach over to grab the vinyl carrying case I keep all my CDs in, I graze the hair on his arm. I find Fleetwood Mac. It's "You Make Loving Fun." I let the pot worm up into my brain, let myself get hungry and eat more pizza. Ron sits up on the floor.

He looks like a little kid. "I'd love to see Brandon and Skyler having a good time at Disney World. First time they've been able to go, and here I am. I just feel like I'm letting them down."

"Janet's just a bitch."

"No. I'm a bastard." He laughs then. Gets a piece of pizza. "Did you know I have a DUI now?" He laughs again.

"No."

"We tried to keep it a secret, but you know, it's public record, so they fired me at the warehouse cause I'm uninsurable. Do you know how fucking hard it is to get a job with a DUI? Don't tell your boss. I'm driving that stock around for him without a damn license."

"I won't. We're paying you out of the drawer anyway," I say.

I move away from him. Sebastian gets up and goes over and sniffs the pizza, helps himself to a bite. I pull him off the pizza and lock him in my bedroom where he will more than likely destroy the bedspread and pillows.

When I come back, Ron is asleep on the floor. I look down at his face in the light from the stereo. His eyes look knotted like two big knuckles. His mouth is twisted in and wet. I kick his ankle softly. His eyes open.

"Better get on the couch," I say. "Your back will hurt like hell in the morning if you sleep on that floor."

He coughs. "Sure." He reaches up and I grab his hand and pull him from the floor. He dives into the couch.

"Goddamn. I'm sleepy," he says. "Thanks."

"For what?"

But he's out again.

+

Janet and the boys are ready to go the next morning. They live in an okay neighborhood right off 562, behind a Kroger's. The suburban two-stories with small yards are rundown, and everybody seems to own the same model of dented-up minivan. I pull in with Sebastian going off in the backseat. The boys are dressed in new shorts, flip-flops and tee-shirts. They're already in the van. Janet's in a big sundress to cover up the weight she's gained. She's the breadwinner—with her job at Lane Bryant, chief bill-collector. Get her on the phone, she will make you pay.

I take Sebastian out, hold him by his leash. But he still manages to jump up on the minivan. Brandon sticks his arms out and tries to grab Sebastian's head.

"Motherfucker!" Brandon yells.

"Shut up," Skyler says. He's sitting in the front passenger seat, rolling his eyes.

Sebastian barks and jumps. I pull back on the leash and run him to the back yard, to the gate. I tie his leash to a low tree limb for the time being. I go back upfront. Janet tells both boys that this is going to be a fun trip, but that she's still trying to get over their dad, so they better be on the best behavior. She has kinky, newly permed hair and purple sunglasses.

"Right, Denny? Tell them."

I look in the windshield and smile. "You better obey her," I say.

Brandon is giving us the finger. He gets ornery when he has something to look forward to. Skyler looks back at him and gives us the finger too, like out of solidarity, even though most of the time he can't stand Brandon.

"Stop it," Janet says, but she starts laughing, and I laugh too. They make a big show of their middle fingers, wagging them and shaking them.

Janet looks over at me, and gives me the key.

"Don't you let him come over, you hear me?" she whispers. "He tell you about the DUI?"

"Last night."

She laughs.

"What are you his new best friend?"

"Maybe his only."

Janet gets into the car. The boys have turned the radio to the rap station. She starts the car, and looks out at me.

"I got you some of them Lean Cuisines we like," she says.

"Thanks."

She pulls out. I go back to make sure Sebastian's okay. The leash is off the limb, and he's heading right to the rusted fence in back. I go get him and try to calm him down. When I finally get him to stop galloping, I turn and see Ron standing in the middle of the yard. He's in shorts and a tank-top and tennis shoes, holding a great big stainless-steel coiled spike in his right hand.

"He'll need to be tied up to something, right? I bet he can jump over that damn fence," Ron says, business-like.

"Yeah. Thanks. I tied him to a tree, but it didn't work."

All the grass is pretty well scorched. There's a pile of action figures next to an overturned barbecue grill. The sun's beating down. He goes to the garage and gets a spade and hacks out a place under a tree to put the spike. I hold onto Sebastian. He's jerking back and forth. I have such a feeling of hatred for Sebastian sometimes, like he is my curse, but then I'll look down at his face and he'll seem almost innocent.

"Try it out," Ron says.

I drag Sebastian over to the spike, and hook his leash up to it. He immediately strains, but the spike holds.

"Good job," I say.

"You eat breakfast?"

"Not yet."

We walk back to the sliding glass doors and into the kitchen, which Janet always keeps spotless. Ron makes omelets. I sit and watch him, feeling guilty because of what Janet said. I look out the sliding glass doors. Sebastian is lying on the ground like he's been given a shot.

"Here you go," Ron says, serving me the omelet.

As I fork the eggs into my mouth, I look over at Ron, and he's looking at me, shell-shocked, like the truth is visiting his brain all of a sudden.

"It's over," he says. He swallows.

"What?"

"My life." He smiles.

"Shut up," I say and laugh.

I get up with my empty plate.

"You know what Janet calls me?" Ron says. He's up now.

"What?"

"A drama queen." Ron puts his plate in the sink with mine.

We go down to the basement where Ron's stereo is. Down here it's almost cold. The floor is carpeted in beige wall-to-wall. There's a black vinyl sofa below a yard-level window and warped paneling on the walls. I hear Sebastian outside barking. Ron turns on his stereo. I lie down on the couch. Fleetwood Mac again, not that loud. The A-C kicks on, a hiss and a belch. Ron moves my legs over so he can sit on the couch. I go down on the floor in front of him.

"Oh, man," Ron whispers.

I unzip him, and after I pull off his shorts I lean on top of him and kiss him deeply. A song goes into a song. Sebastian barks and stops. I taste the inside of his mouth and his skin, warm and vinegary, my hand sliding down his chest and over his small belly, down to his hard-on. When I touch it, I look at his face. His eyes are wide open, focused on the window, like he may need to escape at any minute. His mouth is a sloppy circle from being kissed. I feel like we've been doing this since we were kids.

When we're through, Ron goes up and does dishes. I stay down in the basement for a little bit but eventually I go up. He's in the living room, which Janet doesn't allow anyone to use, its furniture brittle and precious. The lamps are gold angels. He's just standing in the middle of the room, his face as plain as an outer-space alien's.

"I'm taking mental pictures," he says, all intense. "Of every room in this house."

"She'll take you back," I say.

Ron just walks out the front door.

+

Jack's in tonight, while I count money in the office.

"I ordered a keg," he says.

There's just not enough room in the office for a big guy like Jack, so he stands half in and half out, hovering like a magic genie.

"We'll have to watch out. Shane and Darlene aren't twenty-one yet. You invited them, right?"

Jack smiles. "Of course."

"Can't let minors get drunk, okay?" I'm putting bills into paper binders, filling out a deposit slip. Of course it was dead tonight. There's only four days left now. Jack's having a party the last night we're open at his mansion on the hill in Coventry Courts. Tonight, he's wearing a tan jogging suit with sandals. Just had his hair cut, so he looks like an obese businessman in Bermuda.

"You given any thought to my offer?"

"What offer?"

"Management at the Dayton store."

"I don't think I'm going to take it."

I look at Jack's face, and he's trying to keep it cool.

"So what are you going to do?"

I tap in some numbers into the calculator, and a little paper receipt shoots out.

"I'm going to work at Olive Garden."

Jack laughs, all hurt and pissed.

"Olive Garden."

I stand up, zip up the deposit bag. "Excuse me. I gotta close out the drawer."

He follows me to the cash register. There's a smell of ancient mop water and total exhaustion, burnt meat and old walls. Shane, the head cook who's worked here since he was sixteen, is outside waiting for his ride. He's a cute kid with a burr-cut who got arrested last year for drugs in school. Even though he went to juvie for a month, Jack let him have his job back when he got out.

"I'm gonna be a waiter there," I say.

"Shit," Jack says, flabbergasted. "You'll make next to nothing, Denny. I swear to God. I'll give you a raise. You're the best manager I've had."

He's in my face.

"I just want to simplify things."

He laughs again. "Well, move in with me then," he says. It's a joke and it's not.

Shane's ride comes: his grandma in a station wagon. I see the taillights of her car disappear past the strip mall. It's one of those half-foggy August

Next to Nothing

nights. Outside, locking up, holding the deposit bag, I feel happy to be alive, buzzing still from what I did with Ron, even though I know it's trashy. All good things are.

Jack follows me to the night deposit at the bank. When I put the bag into the slot at First National, he honks his horn and tells me to come to his car.

"Let's get a drink," he says.

"I'm too tired."

He likes me to tell him no. That's the way shit works, I know, even though I've never had anybody in hot pursuit of me like this before. And yet for a few seconds out in the bank parking lot, with a bat zooming in and out of a street-light above a Pizza Hut, I feel like I deserve his love because I'm a good person deep down. And I want him to know I'm thankful. But I can't say it.

"You sure?"

"Yeah."

"Well, I'll see you tomorrow probably."

"Okay."

Jack's yellow-green Hummer pulls out onto Route 562.

+

Sebastian is missing.

Ron's spike didn't hold. It's there in the grass, the coiled bottom caked with mud. Ron's standing above it, smoking a cigarette. I light one up and feel the pain I feel at night when I smoke.

"Oh God, Denny, I am so fucking sorry, man," he says. "I went to my lawyer's office and you know, finished up what I could at Pondo. Went and ate. Came back and he was gone right over the fence. I've been all over the neighborhood."

The sorrow in his face isn't about a dog. Deep down I don't really care about Sebastian missing. Well, I do, sort of, but I was going to have to find a place for him anyway. I saved Sebastian from being killed, but that was the only love I had for him, the love of saving his life. After that, I wanted him to disappear.

I look at Ron, and he goes, "Fuck." He's biting his left thumbnail really bad.

"Maybe he'll come back. He's pretty smart," I say.

"Maybe," Ron says. "I'm so sorry."

"That's okay. He'll probably come back."

We do it again around 1:30 in the morning—in his and Janet's bedroom this time. He wants me to fuck him, and I do. It hurts him, but he wants it. I'm thinking he wants to be hurt because he's such a loser—of dogs and his driver's license and his family and his mind, all at the same time. But when I fuck him I also can feel him come out of his body in a way. Maybe the pain is what he needs. I go slow, so slow it's almost like we aren't doing anything, just pretending.

After, he gets up without a word. He goes to the kitchen and I hear the microwave bleep, then the sound of popcorn. I smell the popcorn eventually, and I'll be damned if he hasn't burned it.

+

The Ponderosa Steakhouse on Patterson Boulevard is now officially shut down. Jack's party is tonight. I've let his three other employees go home early to get ready. I change my clothes in the restaurant bathroom, come back out and give the gutted dining room one last look. This is your life, kiddo. Of course I think about Ron in the psych ward. He tried to kill himself the day Janet and the kids got back from Disney. In the basement, with a bottle of Janet's sleeping pills. She found him, saw the note, called 9-1-1.

I arrived in the emergency room, after a very pissed-off Janet called me, just in time to see Ron puke up the charcoal they had given him to absorb what drugs were left after the stomach pumping. Janet left the boys at a neighbor's house. She was sitting in the ER waiting room, still in the stupid bright lavender Minnie Mouse sweatshirt she had gotten herself as a souvenir.

"Why did you let him in the house? I took his key. I know you were the one who let him in the house. I knew he was going to pull some stunt like this. He is so damn manic." She rolled her eyes.

"I'm sorry. Is he going to live?"

"Probably."

She picked up a tattered old *Newsweek* off an end table, started flipping through it. There was an old man across the room, moaning, holding his arms like there was a baby in them. Janet looked up at me.

"He's just about worthless," she said. "I mean, he is the father of my kids, and I love him. But I can't live with him. Especially now."

"I know."

She looked down at the *Newsweek*, like it might have an answer in it to her problem. Even in the waiting room, I still saw Ron in my head the way I always did, like some long-lost love of mine from a dream, and heard that voice from when I was so sick I could barely see, the voice that hovered above Bob Barker's and the music from *Love Boat*: "You remember the chest-busting scene in *Alien*? Did that not fucking blow your mind?"

A fat bald male nurse came out and said, "He wants to see Denny. He asked if Denny was here."

Janet shook her head, still glaring at *Newsweek*, and then gave me the evil eye. She knew exactly what Ron and I had done. She wasn't mad or anything, just disgusted.

"Go on," she whispered to herself. "Go baby him. I'm sick of it."

Ron was grinning like he'd just played a silly joke on everyone, his lips black from the charcoal. Tubes came out from a catheter and from his neck.

"I ain't got insurance," he said.

"Who does?"

He laughed.

"I like you," he said.

He spat some black shit out of his mouth. An infomercial played on TV. The walls were scuffed-up and beige. I could smell pee and whatever they use in hospitals to hide the smell of pee. My stomach hurt. I wanted to kiss him.

"I like you too," I said.

+

He lives in a million-dollar mansion on a hill in a part of the county that's got a bunch of brand new, huge homes. Jack not only owns restaurants, but has also made a killing manufacturing the speed they sell in little glow-in-the-dark packages next to the cash register at convenience stores. Old-looking cars are parked at odd angles outside. Inside all the lights are on. California-colored walls and leather furniture and glassy surfaces. Black balloons and a cardboard tombstone with PONDEROSA 1975—2005 RIP on it. There is an END OF THE UNIVERSE cake on Beef Stroganoff's big dining-room table.

Jack's in the back of the kitchen, making Bloody Marys. I can tell he's trying to seduce little Shane. Jack has on a maroon velour jogging outfit and leather sandals.

"Denny!" he yells, cutting off a stalk of celery.

"I made it."

Somebody is playing "Last Dance" by Donna Summer on a boombox. All the tired employees are drinking and laughing in Jack's living room. Nobody dances. Everybody smokes.

"Yes, you did. Hey, Shane, hon, could you take this out to Phyllis?"

Shane laughs. "Sure." He's wearing a tee-shirt with a big "3" with angel wings on it.

"I want to talk to you," Jack says. "Come on."

Drunker than hell, Jack opens the backdoor and stumbles out to a luxurious built-in pool, with lights at the bottom, glowing like a spaceship that's been inserted into concrete. No one else is in sight. Jack walks next to the pool's edge, drinking from his tumbler of Bloody Mary.

"I'm giving you one last chance," he says, turning around, facing me.

"What?"

"I want you to be my lead manager at the Pondo in Dayton," he says, but then his gaze hits the water. He seems like he wants to jump in.

"No," he says. "Not just that. I want you to move in here with me." His laugh is a poker-party laugh.

When he comes at me for his kiss, I feel like we both might just float up into the air and disappear, but I fall into the pool instead. I take in a huge gulp of water, flail and start sinking down to the bottom. Tomorrow I'm supposed to pick up Ron at the hospital. He'll be waiting on me and I'll be dead. I'll have done what he wanted to do to himself. I'll be successful at what he tried to do. It's funny in a way.

Suddenly I'm jerked up and out of the water. Someone flips me onto the concrete. Jack hovers. People come out. It's a real hoot. I'm hacking and gagging myself right back into life. I wind up on Jack's bed. His bedroom is major-deluxe: all cool green walls and satiny sheets. Shane is standing by a chrome-lined dresser, lighting up a crack pipe. He sucks in like a baby kitten.

"He wanted me to watch you," he says, slowly opening his eyes.

"Jack?"

"Yeah." Shane laughs. "Don't tell anybody about this." He shakes the blue-glass pipe at me.

I get up, fevered and tired, but not really that out of it for someone who almost just drowned. I smell the leftover tang of Shane's crack.

"We didn't call an ambulance or nothing. Jack was afraid about the drugs. Do you think you need to go to the emergency room?"

Shane puts his pipe down on a dresser, and sits beside me. I don't know anything about him, except that he would always work double-shifts for me when somebody called in sick. A crack-smoking get-along kind of guy, always willing to help out.

"No. I'm fine. I feel stupid."

I smile at him. Shane smiles back. His eyes are the color of a Magic 8 Ball before the little green square floats up to tell you your future.

"I'm gonna miss closing with you," he says.

"Me too."

Shane extends his hand and shakes mine. We hug. I feel a flood of emotion bigger than Jack's pool bursting out of my stomach and heart. I pull myself away from him, stand up, turn around.

"You sure you're okay? You want me to go get Jack? He's pretty fucked up though. That guy can't stop saying he loves you. He's telling everybody."

"No. No." I'm laughing now. "Don't worry about it. I need a cigarette."

Shane pulls one from his shirt pocket and lights it for me. My lungs catch fire.

"Life sure is funny," I whisper.

"What?" Shane says.

+

I pick up Ron the next morning, dressed in my Olive Garden outfit because it's my first day of work. He's ready in the dayroom, with his plaid suitcase, dressed in the jeans and tee-shirt he tried to kill himself in.

"I'm all signed out," he says. His eyes sparkle like two chemicals mixing. He is happy. He has the shakes.

"Let's go."

He's going to stay with me. Soon he'll have hospital bills up to his ass. He'll file for bankruptcy. But today he's out and maybe there's hope in the morning air. Ron has prescriptions, so we stop at the Walgreens. I wait on him in the car. He comes out with three white bags, shaking them in front of the windshield.

"It's like trick or treat." He laughs kind of sheepishly, embarrassed, gets in. "I had to use my MasterCard. So you actually are gonna do this Olive Garden thing?"

We pull out.

"Today's the first day I'm on a shift for real."

He's eyeing the Waffle House now as we sit at a stoplight.

"Man, I'm starved."

I pull in, get out and wait on him as he hides his new meds under the front seat. He seems shorter and skinnier. He still wears his white plastic hospital bracelet. I know I'll be working my ass off to help him. There will be days when I'll come home after pulling a double shift and he'll be eating a grilled cheese sandwich in his underwear watching *The A-Team*. I know this. Part of the joy of loving him is the sacrifice I am making, that feeling of giving up everything to get just one thing you want back in return. Almost like voodoo, like selling your soul so you can have one.

We sit in a booth and order. Mostly it's truckers and the women who love them around us. I smell burnt batter and grease.

"I've got like forty-five minutes," I say.

"We'll eat fast."

The waitress is pretty good—gets the order out in no time. Ron eats like he just got out of prison.

"Maybe I can get on at Olive Garden too. Dishwasher or something."

"Yeah, maybe," I say.

We finish up and go outside. The heat has already started to turn rancid. I'm about to get in the car when Ron lets out a big yell from the other side.

"Look over there!" he says, pointing across the road to a strip mall with a closed record store, a furniture place, and a Hobby Lobby. Next to the poles of a big sign is a skinny gray ghost of a dog, long snout, panting hard as he smells the air. It's Sebastian. It just has to be.

Ron runs to the highway. I stay put. Cars honk and pass as he works his way across the road. As soon as Sebastian sees Ron, he starts to run the other way toward a fence, beyond which are train tracks, trees and weeds. He's running for his life from a mad man. Ron whistles and waves his arms.

"Come here baby! Hey Sebastian! Hey! Come back!"

I get in the car. Start the engine. Turn on the A-C.

Just Let Me Have This

Robert's mom turned lesbian last year, two weeks after her fifty-third birthday, then divorced his dad around the same time. She and her lady friend organized a commitment ceremony to take place at the Edgewood State Park lodge, over on the Ohio/Indiana border. Robert was going. He was thirty-two years old. At first, the revelation about his mom made him feel disgusted and pissed. But he got over it. Plus she kept loaning him money, so he couldn't bitch.

The night before the ceremony, Robert was standing in front of the Wendy's where he worked, after getting off. It was the middle of April but hot. A gas station and a little strip mall were going up next to the Wendy's. They were half-done and dredged-up looking. Dad's car arrived and Robert got in. Soon wind was blowing in through the open driver-side window and lifting up Dad's comb-over. Robert watched and felt the top of his own head and the bald spot there.

Dad eventually pulled into the parking lot of the Blue Circle, a closed-down drive-in restaurant near downtown he had just got a small business loan to buy. In front was a line of parking spaces under a bright blue tarp, and in each space was a little menu-stand covered in a black garbage bag and duct-tape. The circular blue stucco restaurant itself had tinted windows.

Dad made a big deal out of unlocking the front door, like he was doing a magic trick. The smell inside the place was mildew and mouse-shit. Three cash-registers sat on a stainless steel counter, and above them was a big Blue Circle menu board with prices from 1989, when it had shut down.

Behind the counter, Dad picked up a cellophane-wrapped plastic tub of cleaners and paper towels and other janitorial supplies. It had a big blue bow.

"Your mom got this for me. I brought her out here this morning," he said.

Blue Circle had been the only hangout for high-school kids back when Dad and Mom were kids. They used to cruise the parking lot on Saturday nights, smoking cigarettes and drinking Cherry Cokes, acting out all their big dramas. Way before the divorce, Dad wanted to buy the place. He always talked about what a gold mine it was, how a lot of people in this town had fond memories of it, how they could bring their kids blah-blah-blah. But later it became a place where he went to forget about the fact that Mom had left him. Plus the paper plant where he worked for twenty-four years offered him early retirement.

"That's a real nice gift," Robert said. He knew the tone to take.

"When's your car going to be done?" Dad said, opening up the cellophane and pulling out a bottle of Windex.

"They said to stop by around 7:00." Robert looked at his watch: 6:30 PM. He had a 1996 Dodge Omni and it was paid off but falling apart (bad alternator this time). He was thinking about getting another car, but that would be hard, especially because of the child support.

Dad sprayed Windex all over a window in the back, wiped real hard and showed Robert what had come off the glass. Robert got some Formula 409 from the gift tub and started spraying the tops of the cash registers. They cleaned together for about ten minutes. Recently Dad had been hinting about Robert quitting Wendy's and teaming up with him at the Blue Circle. But Robert got manager last year. He was making okay money for someone without a four-year college degree. And being with Dad all the time seemed to Robert like a way for them to end up hating each other the rest of their lives. That was something they couldn't afford to let happen.

Finally Robert said, "Hey. We gotta go get my car."

Dad came up to him, eyes shiny and stubborn, putting his Windex bottle back into the gift tub.

"Root beer floats," he said like it was the title to his favorite song. "Root beer floats. I'm gonna put them back on the menu here. You ever had a good old fashioned root beer float?"

"I guess," Robert said.

Dad stood there, still smiling. He almost said something else, but started whistling instead. Robert imagined himself shooting his dad in the head, like putting an animal out of its misery. He felt bad about that, so he smiled back.

Dad said it one more time: "Root beer float."

Then they left.

+

Hannah was Robert's seven-year-old daughter. She lived with his ex-wife and his ex-wife's mom in Lexington, Kentucky. He used to talk to her on the phone but hadn't in over three years. He didn't talk to Rita, his ex-wife, anymore either.

When Robert first met Rita, at the bar near the plastics plant where he worked before it shut down, she wasn't really fat, just round-faced and plump, kind of curvy. He had seen her out of the corner of his eye as he did karaoke to "Enter Sandman" by Metallica, drunk and happy, getting louder and louder. She would stare at him and grin big, then look away. She told him after their second date it was love at first sight and he said, "Same here."

He'd spent seven years partying and going from job to job after high school. So when he met Rita, he just figured it was time to get married. Plus she seemed to want him so much.

The thing that really bothered him the most about being married to Rita was her getting up in the middle of the night to eat whatever she could find. She'd done it since she was a little girl, she told him. It got going full-force during her pregnancy, which made sense, but then it got even worse after Hannah was born. One time he got out of bed and found her out in the hall

Just Let Me Have This

popping big-sized marshmallows into her mouth, one right after the other. She had no idea she was being watched. If she had though, he imagined her saying: *Leave me alone. Quit looking. Just let me have this.*

Then one night Rita said, "Gosh, I'm hungry."

They were about to go out on a "date." Rita's best friend had offered to baby-sit. Hannah was one year old. Rita was standing by the entertainment center his mom and dad had bought them, dressed in a skirt that didn't fit right because of her weight. Robert was trying to watch TV and Rita laughed in that little-girl way of hers.

"You hungry too?" Rita said.

She wanted him to be like he was in the bar when she first saw him, he knew: fun-loving and drunk because he had Monday off.

"How about that one place that makes that chicken you like?" she asked, trying to be nice.

Robert stood up and hit her across the face, knocked her down. She did not make a sound.

He left and came back around 2:00 in the morning to find her sitting on the couch in the same outfit except she'd put on a pair of tube-socks because of the cold. He felt so miserable that he just burst into tears. Rita looked at him like he was invisible. Hannah started crying and Rita went to her. He sat down on the floor beside the entertainment center and looked up and saw Rita rocking Hannah in their bedroom. He remembered earlier that morning Hannah's eyes looking up at him as he changed her diaper. The love he felt coming from her was like a tickle in his throat he was afraid would become a lump that could choke him for good. Then again Hannah was all he had that meant anything.

Robert got up off the floor. He went to Rita, and kissed Hannah's head.

Rita forgave him. He only hit her two more times after that. But one day, when Hannah was four, Rita said she was done with it all. He hadn't really gotten to know Hannah that well anyway, working two jobs (so they could rent a house), hiding from the both of them.

When Rita and Hannah went to Lexington to live with her mom, he helped move their stuff. The divorce went through. He started paying child support, which was taken out of his paycheck; that way he would never forget and was never tempted to skip. And sometimes he would look at his paycheck stub and see the child support deduction and it would make him proud in a way—proud to have done something for them, instead of hiding and apologizing and being pissed all the time. But when he wasn't looking at his check stub, it was hard not to forget about them.

+

Six hundred eighty-seven dollars for his car to get fixed. At least it had started in the morning and he had gotten to work okay. Now it was almost 3:30 PM. Dressed in a black suit with a maroon necktie and white shirt, he looked at himself in the Wendy's men's room mirror. He'd shaved his head in the morning. It took a while. He used a disposable razor and nicked himself a couple times, starting with his bald spot and working his way in circles around his scalp. He could still see a few pinpricks above his forehead, little red stars.

On his way out, Charity, the girl running the cash register, said, "Pretty slick."

Charity had clocked in while he was changing. She had a nose-ring that some other managers had issues with, but Robert didn't give a crap as long as she showed up for her shift. Plus they had fucked the other night after everybody had gone home. It was real quick, in the stockroom. She was so skinny he felt like he was killing her. But they smoked pot in his car and did it one more time at his apartment. The next day his alternator went out, and he had to call Triple A.

While waiting for a cab, Charity told him, "You look so sad."

"Well, my fucking car…"

Then he grunted at her like she was being a dumb-ass. They were on his couch, watching TV. It was raining. She had on her Wendy's uniform from last night. She leaned over and kissed his cheek.

"No, I mean really sad," she whispered. The silver nose-ring glowed against the paleness of her upper lip. Her long dark hair was pulled back behind her ears.

"I'm okay," he said. He wanted her to go so bad.

There was a honk outside. She kissed him again and got up and went out the door. He thought about Hannah. Having a kid and not knowing her—maybe that's what Charity saw on his face, even though he didn't think he was thinking about it.

"Got a hot date?" Charity asked now. She was wiping down trays next to the cash register, which was surrounded by little purple robot dolls that came with kids' meals.

"Yeah. Hot date," Robert said. He had not told a soul about his mom's gay wedding.

"Well, I hope you have a really good time," she said.

He made eye contact with her then. Charity stared right back.

"I will," he said.

"Fuck you."

"Nice language." He laughed, but went toward the door.

He thought about firing her, or at least telling Jerry the manager on-duty about what she'd done. But they'd have to call somebody to cover her shift, plus she would go ballistic and tell Jerry he was fucking her and smoking pot with her. So he just left.

+

It took about an hour to get to Edgewood State Park. The lodge was a glass-fronted A-frame, half dark wood and half red brick, at the center of the park. Its reception area had flat green carpet and dark paneled walls. No one was at the front desk. He just wandered past it and heard some laughing down at the end of the hallway.

The hallway opened onto an enclosed balcony with huge windows show-ing the lake and surrounding woods. The sun coming off the lake almost hurt his eyes. He stood for a second until he heard his mom yell from down below.

"Get down here and help us, Robbie!"

From the landing Robert saw his mom and Terri, Mom's lady friend, and some lady with short red hair in a short skirt. All of them were rearranging tables and chairs. Mom was in a white sun dress, and she looked a little red (she had been going to a tanning booth recently). Her hair was cut spiky and short. Robert walked down the steps to the sunlit ballroom. There was the same green wall-to-wall, the same dark paneling, but part of the floor was wood-parquet for dancing. To the left was an eight-stool bar nestled in between arcade machines, and to the right was the door to an indoor pool.

Mom came over to him. It was like being a big lesbian and meeting Terri had given her a whole new outgoing personality. Or maybe she was truly happy and Robert had never witnessed this before. While he was growing up, both his parents worked all the time, and when they did things together, like eating out or even going to Florida that one time, they were like people shoved together for some purpose that had not yet been explained to them and probably never would.

"The tables were set up all wrong," Terri said from behind Mom in her low-pitched voice. She hugged Robert.

"We wanted a horse-shoe pattern," Mom said. She frowned. "You shaved your head, Robbie."

"Yeah," Robert said.

The red-headed woman came over. She looked a little like Terri but she was taller and skinnier. She wore a lot of makeup like a co-host on a morning show. Her skirt was short and black, and she had on a dark purple top and black high heels.

Terri said, "Hey Wanda—this is Robert, Doris's son. Robert, this is my sister Wanda."

"He shaved all his hair off!" Mom said to Wanda. "And he's so skinny!"

Wanda looked right at him. "I like that look." She grinned big and her teeth looked artificial white.

"I don't know. It makes you look mean," Mom said. "Like a skinhead." She smiled though.

"He looks handsome," Terri said, laughing, but then she coughed (from cigarettes).

"I guess." Mom sounded worried, but then went over and kissed his cheek and thanked him for coming.

Mom and Terri went back to the tables. Robert looked up at Wanda and she was staring at him. He felt good about it, almost like he was someplace else in a different situation.

"You don't look mean to me," Wanda said.

+

About ten people showed up in all, people Mom worked with at the bakery in the mall and Terri worked with at the insurance office. They had a Native American woman do their ceremony, Donna Stark-Feather. She had a switch from a tree, and she had them blow onto its leaves. Robert sat next to Wanda. He still felt her looking at him.

Donna Stark-Feather said, "These two beautiful women stand before you today proclaiming their love."

In her skinny jean skirt and feathery vest and half-glasses, Donna Stark-Feather waved the switch around both of them like a magic wand. After they kissed at the end, and the two of them opened their eyes, Mom and Terri looked like two little kids, completely relieved that nobody had ruined their fun. Robert tried to think of his mom as who she used to be—married to his dad, sitting in their old house in her housecoat, drowsy at 7:30 PM, watching *Entertainment Tonight* or some such shit.

"They make a cute couple, don't they?" Wanda said to him.

Robert nodded. "I'm happy for her," he said, lowering the pitch in his voice to sound sincere.

Maybe it was the tone in his voice, but Wanda laughed and said, "You sure you're okay with your mom being a lesbian?"

He said it didn't bother him. She stopped laughing and looked like she was trying to believe him. He was trying to believe what he said too. Mom and Terri were both talking to a few of their friends while Donna Stark-Feather took a big long gulp from her bottle of water. They looked like they had no idea how disgusting they were. What upset Robert the most was the fact that Mom was happy being a person he did not know. She was betraying him by turning into this over-friendly, fake-tan lesbian. Though he had to admit to himself he had never really known her that well in the first place.

Dad turned up around 7:30 PM. He didn't say anything to anybody, which he did sometimes, just showed up places and stayed in the background like he'd been hired as a movie extra. Robert saw him by the pool doors in a sweater, pants and sneakers, looking around.

The food was on silver dishes over Sterno burners, next to stacks of white china plates and cylinders of silverware. The round tables were covered in maroon cloths. There were Swedish meatballs and chicken wings and broccoli with cheese sauce. The lodge workers (three women and one man) were friendly and speedy. Mom and Terri sat with Robert and Wanda.

"Dad's here," Robert said, wiping his mouth on a cloth napkin, which to him felt like he was wiping his mouth on a coat.

"I invited him. He should have something to eat," Mom said. Her face got serious. "I want us all to be friends."

Wanda said, "Is he mad about you two?"

"No, he's fine with it. I think he knew deep down for quite a while," Mom said. "That it was over between us, I mean."

Mom then looked at Robert, scared that he might say something snide. But he kept his mouth shut.

"He took me over to the Blue Circle place he bought," Mom said. "I hope that works out for him."

"He's really into it," Robert said.

"Blue Circle?" Wanda said. "I used to hang out there all the time. God— years ago. It's been closed for years."

"My dad's reopening it," Robert said, looking down at the floor. He could not eat what he'd put on his plate.

"Good for him," Wanda said.

Mom and Terri got up because one of the lodge workers had brought out a sheet cake. They did their toast and started handing out the cake to everyone. The deejay showed up. He was a short guy in a maroon leather jacket, playing mostly country songs.

Wanda asked Robert to get a drink at the bar with her.

"I need something a little stronger than this," she said, shaking her plastic cup of wine.

"Sure."

One of the lady lodge workers who'd put out the food was the bartender. Robert ordered a beer, and Wanda said she wanted a White Russian. They drank both really quickly and then ordered more. There was a basketball game on the big-screen TV.

A few kids were hanging out by the pool doors. They were looking past Robert and giggling. He turned and saw that Mom and Terri were on the parquet dancing real close.

Then Wanda yelled over at the kids: "Get a fucking life!"

They ran off.

Wanda lit up a cigarette and he asked if he could have one.

"Smoke them so I won't," Wanda said.

She seemed so sane and good-natured. She told him that she sold Mary Kay Cosmetics for a living, and he said he bet that she was a big success. Her cigarettes were menthols and made his head feel heavy. They ordered more drinks.

It got dark.

Robert looked out at the dance-floor. There Dad was, out of nowhere, with Terri. His face was blank but he was trying to fit in, smiling and looking like he was in on a joke they were playing on him. Wanda was rubbing Robert's left thigh real tender. Her fingers slowly crawled up his thigh, until he stopped them with his fingers, and she laced her fingers through his. He liked the feeling of catching her and being caught by her at the same time.

Robert wasn't sure when he and Wanda started doing shots. But now Wanda threw her head back real dramatically as she drank from one of those sour apple test-tubes. Robert did his the same way. After Wanda touched his leg again, she leaned in close and kissed his forehead. Robert slid off the bar-stool.

"Bathroom," he said.

He thought he might have to puke, but as he walked the feeling went away. The indoor pool area was humid, a few kids and a couple adults were in the pool, and everything—the pool and people and blue concrete—seemed made out of melting rubber. His brain felt like a big juicy knot of nothing.

Robert walked into the bathroom. Dad was at the sink, splashing water onto his face. The water had gotten into his comb-over, making the strands of hair sink into his eyes like baby tentacles. Robert went to a stall and peed.

Dad was still there with the water running after Robert finished.

"Pretty good reception, huh?" Dad's voice sounded like it had come from a ventriloquist's shut mouth.

Robert smiled into the mirror at Dad while he washed his hands. But he wanted to close his eyes. Dad pushed back the comb-over so that it was again on top of his scalp. Then he touched Robert's arm. His fingers were wet. Robert turned to him, hoping Dad wasn't going to cry. Robert was too drunk to deal with that. But Dad was not crying. He looked mad, and he glared right into Robert's eyes like he was trying to solve a dangerous mystery. Then he looked back into the mirror.

"I don't know what to do," Dad said to the mirror. He was breaking down all the way now, closing his eyes real tight and holding onto the sink like he might fall down and never get up again.

Robert left. He walked past the people and the pool, back out to the bar, where Wanda was ordering more drinks, past her, and he walked out onto the dance-floor. Just a few people were left. Mom and Terri were dancing together, real close, to some song by Wynonna. Seeing them, he felt like a kid who'd been abandoned—like some little fucker whose parents dropped him off at the mall and never came back to get him.

"Robbie," Mom said over Terri's shoulder. She was dopey-looking from getting what she wanted. Robert thought about all those years she spent with Dad when really she wanted some lady in her bed.

"Robbie, you want to dance with your dear old mom?"

He walked over and Terri pulled back and there Mom was in front of him.

"You fucking dyke," Robert said to his mom. "You make me sick."

Mom's face seemed caught, like she was trapped in an elevator going down real fast. He grabbed her. He felt powerful and started to shake her like you might shake somebody to wake her up. Mom was telling him to stop. She was pretty big, but she was like a little kid as he shook her. He wanted to pick her up and throw her, but then that feeling stopped and he stopped.

Terri yelled, "Let go of her!"

Wanda came over and pulled on him. Mom walked backwards, her eyes closed. Then she opened them. For the first time in his life it looked like she hated him for real.

"Get out of here," she said, real loud.

+

"It's got to be complicated for a guy having a lesbian for a mom," Wanda said in her room that she had at the lodge. She'd told Robert earlier that she got it because she knew she was going to get blitzed. She always got blitzed at weddings, gay or not, she said.

"You didn't have to call her that name." All of a sudden Wanda looked sad. Maybe even judgmental. It truly was not a good mix—her being so drunk and sad and judgmental. Wanda was red and sweaty in the face.

"I mean. You physically assaulted her sort of. She looked so pitiful," Wanda said, but then she laughed too, which made Robert want to leave. She stopped laughing.

"I know what you need," she said, almost like she was going to punish him.

She got down on her knees and unbuckled his pants. He just stood there. The bed was covered in a satin spread. There was an entertainment center and a desk. He couldn't get hard. Wanda tried biting at it, licking it softly, everything. But he could not get it up. She stopped, fell back a little, and then stood up.

"You need to apologize to your mother," she said. She was making direct eye contact, like this was the last time she would ever do that. Then she ran into the bathroom.

Robert zipped his pants up and walked to the bathroom door. It was wide open. Wanda was bent over the commode. All her beauty products and stuff were lined up real neat on the sink area. She looked up from the toilet and gave him a dirty look and was about to say something but then she had to vomit again.

"You need any help or anything?" he heard himself say. He wanted to please her suddenly. He wanted to help her through whatever this was.

Wanda got up after she finished. He helped her to bed. She was quiet and almost ready to collapse, but she thanked him in a whisper. He covered her up, pulling the bedspread up to her chin. She was out. He got into the bed on the other side. It was late as hell, and he was tired. He felt like he was about to get sick himself, but he closed his eyes against it. He thought of Rita when she helped him when he was real bad sick one time, food poisoning from takeout pizza. He saw Rita's round concerned face. She had a damp washcloth ready for his head and she'd gone out and gotten ginger ale and 7-Up and stuff like that. She was in her dark blue housecoat and her hair was cut short. She was big then. Probably morbidly obese. Hannah was staying all night with some little girl in the neighborhood. It was the night before Rita left him.

After Robert got up from the floor, Rita helped him into bed. She tucked him in without saying one word. She put a glass of 7-up on the side table, and got a plastic bucket just in case.

In the bed, Robert closed his eyes. He felt better, even though he knew he would have to puke again in a few minutes. He felt better with Rita standing there over him. But then he remembered those few times he'd hit her, seeing her pitiful and afraid and stuck. When she would get up, her face was always stubborn, like she was ready to kill him but she couldn't, like she only wanted to get away from him and yet she knew she was always the one who had to help him too.

"Thank you," Robert whispered, with his eyes closed. "I mean really. Thank you."

"You're welcome," Rita whispered.

She was his wife. He loved her, but he knew he would only love her for those few seconds he realized he needed her.

From Me to You

I

Soon as she gets comfortable in Dad's old La-Z-Boy, Lisa asks if we have any eggnog.

"Lisa, honey, it's August," Mom says from over on the couch.

"So?" Lisa is in a pair of skintight jeans and a pink turtleneck with no sleeves. She is so fat now that you almost can't tell it's her. She has not been back here with us in fifteen years.

"Eggnog is for Christmas." Mom tries to smile. She has on a maroon house-coat and a pair of my tube socks. Her black hair is a tad greasy. She's been too tired to bathe of late.

"I could go out and see if I can find some," I say. I'm in the kitchen doorway between the two rooms.

Lisa turns her head towards me and laughs real loud.

"You're a gentleman. You are a true gentle man! This is my little brother, and he is a true gentleman! He lives here with my momma and they love each other!"

She's talking to Dean, the husband she brought with her, who has the face of the skinny guy in the *Laurel and Hardy* movies. He has on a short-sleeved shirt with a clip-on necktie and jeans and cowboy boots.

It takes a little time for Lisa to get up from the recliner. But once she is up, she stumbles over and hugs me. Her whole body feels mushy as wet bread. Like you could push your fingers right through her.

I smile as she breaks away. I love her like you might love a stubbed toe if the rest of your body was numb.

"You don't have to go out and get it, darling," she whispers, taking her time.

Lisa then sits down on the opposite side of the room in the wicker chair that makes sounds like knuckles cracking. She peers out the window tragically. Suddenly it looks like she has two black eyes. Dean stands guard next to her.

"I needed to come home," Lisa says to the window. "I just needed to come home is all."

"Well, that's good," Mom says.

There's silence. Lisa's eyelids drop down, and we watch her go to sleep in the wicker chair. Her hair looks like it has been burned white, and her face resembles a flat tire. But it's still her. You can tell Dean has found meaning in his life by simply standing beside Lisa. I think he told us he sells used car parts for a living.

"She loves you all," Dean whispers. He swallows real hard.

2

When I was little, Lisa used to dress me up like a girl. We started in her bedroom, which had glossy peach walls and a full-length mirror with lipstick peace signs on it. Me: her littlest brother in a pretty sundress and headscarf ensemble, skinny and pale, walking through the house into the backyard. I liked the attention, pretending to be a dressed-up girl out where the three plum trees used to be. Led Zeppelin was usually playing through the speaker balanced on Lisa's window sill.

This one time, close to sundown, we made a picnic: Pringles, plums and tap water. Lisa smoked Dad's cigarettes. We were all alone. Marty, our brother, was out breaking his arm somewhere. Mom was at church, and Dad was at the radio station playing easy-listening music and talking about current events with callers-in.

Lisa said, "He's doing it to you isn't he?"

The only house near us was the one that burnt down. We were on the edge of a little woods right where the mountains start.

"No." A plum squished between my toes. It smelled like honey and arm-pits.

Lisa laughed. "Dancing Days" came from the window. Our house was sloppy looking and built-onto, a chicken-coop mansion Dad inherited from his dad, Zero, who made a living cutting down trees. Zero was always gone, Dad told us. He practically had to raise himself because his mom was deli-cate and secretive and she eventually died of pneumonia one spring when he was eleven.

"Do you even know what I'm talking about?" Lisa said.

I did. She meant Dad coming into the big room they'd given me, the one with the big sleigh bed and bookshelves filled with Grandpa Zero's encyclo-pedias. My room, but nothing in it was mine except some clothes and toys. Dad came in and slipped into the bed, put his hand over my face. Then it was like I was nothing but a part of the bed he was using, and when I screamed there was the hand. After, he went down the hall and did the same thing to Marty. The next day it was bacon and eggs and his great big stereo in the living room playing "Moon River."

"I saw it the other morning," Lisa said. "I was coming out of the bathroom and I saw it. I mean, I always knew there was something weird with him and you two, but I'd never seen it in the light of day."

Lisa got closer. She was skinny and beautiful and her hair was like a lion's mane. She put black stuff all over her eye lashes.

"It hurts when he does it, doesn't it?" she whispered. She looked mad at me.

I looked down at the plum spurting between my toes. I couldn't talk. When he did it, it was like a match being struck against my spine.

From Me to You

"I'll kill the motherfucker," Lisa said. She went in and changed the record to Pink Floyd.

Eventually Dad pulled up in his Cadillac, an armful of records, a thermos. He had golden hair he sprayed into a dome, and a gut from drinking whole milk and eating Reese's Cups while watching *Bewitched*. He took one look at me in my get-up and laughed.

"Why do you keep dressing him up like this?" he asked Lisa. "He's not your little doll."

Lisa was pulling weeds over by the broken-down car. He came over to me and told me to take the records. I did.

"Hey," Dad yelled at Lisa.

She looked up.

"What?"

Her eyes got the light from the kitchen window. The Pink Floyd music was like dirty water spilling out of pipes into a lake.

"Why do you keep dressing him like this? That could mentally scar him."

Sometimes Dad stayed in the bathtub for six hours at a stretch, dumped seven or eight bottles of isopropyl alcohol into steaming hot water and soaked till it cooled to lukewarm soup. I was always hoping he was in there crying like a girl.

"You shut the fuck up, pervert," Lisa said. She kept pulling weeds.

He looked embarrassed and scared, walking over to her. It took a little time to squat down because of his knees. "What?"

The record albums I was holding got heavy. One was about to drop.

"You heard me."

"I want you to get up and go to your room," he says.

"I know what you're doing to them, Daddy." She looked right at him then, like her eyes could kill him.

Dad stood up and looked at me and smiled, like, *Look, Lisa's gone off the deep end again.*

"I know what you do to them!" That one was a scream.

Even then I knew Lisa felt left out because of what he did to us, like it was a game she could not be a part of and she was jealous and wanted to be let in so she could be emotionally torn up too.

Lisa stood up and ran into the house. Dad went in. I dropped all the records, and after I picked them up, I stood by the back screen door. I heard Dad in there yelling but trying to laugh too:

"We're not having this. We're not. We are not having this. You need to calm down. You need to get some manners."

I heard Lisa scream and grunt. When I went in, they were both on the living room floor, Lisa sobbing and beating at Dad real hard, and Dad trying to hold onto her, trying to get her to stop.

3

Mom got cancer last year. I had to make her go to the doctor. She's always been a big gal, and losing all the weight has turned her timid and home-bound. She has started going through all Zero's encyclopedias, and is always looking up gaunt-eyed and stiff from one of those big green books, telling me about what she's discovered.

"Did you know that in 1962 the average salary for an adult male in Argentina was five hundred dollars per year?" She looks lost, like she might need to make a retreat from all words after saying that.

"No, Mom, I didn't." I laugh.

I am all she has left, and she's all I have left. Sounds more depressing than it really is.

4

Now Lisa is in a housecoat, sipping coffee the next day after her homecoming. Last night, she finally woke up in the wicker chair, refreshed and yawning. I went out and picked up some Kentucky Fried. We all stayed up watching movies on the VCR, ones Dad had left behind—*The Money Pit* and *The Sunshine Boys* and *Imitation of Life*. All the way through Mom slept and Dean kept watch on Lisa and Lisa kept going to the bathroom to drink and I sat through all the movies like I always do, my eyes so open they turned into plums. The movies blurred into each other, like real life. Lisa got so drunk finally she whispered to me in the dark.

"I should have never left you here."

"I'm okay."

I looked over at her. She was on the couch with her big face shining in the TV light almost like an albino jack-o-lantern. You could still see the pretty in it though, the wild pretty she had when she was sixteen and always wanting to kill herself.

"It kills me," she whispered, and then she dropped off.

I could not believe it but Dean, stick-thin and wasted-looking, picked her up like a little girl is picked up by her daddy. He just went over and lifted her right up. Obviously he was used to it. He grunted and carried her off to bed.

Lisa is silent now. Morning sun shimmers through the windows. Dean is at the sink doing her pills. He turns around and gives the dispenser to her, wordless and calm. Lisa opens the first compartment, takes a few with her coffee.

"You going to the store?" she asks Dean like we aren't even there. Her voice is raspy, a little paw digging through dirt.

Dean nods his head.

"I'll make a list."

She goes over to her purse and drops everything out, like an actress in a serious movie about mental illness. All kinds of stuff falls out, packages of cookies and a bottle of Diet Mountain Dew Code Red and four or five hair brushes and a Ziploc baggie of make-up. She finds paper and pen and writes down what she wants.

Dean looks at the list. He frowns.

"Please," she says. But it's not like she's begging, it's like she's getting ready to do something that will make you want to die.

"Mom has a doctor's appointment," I tell them. "We could stop off at the store after it, if Dean has something else to do."

Dean nods. "No," he says. "Thanks, but I'll do it."

"I'm taking a bath today," Lisa says, her eyes going wide. "A big old decadent bubble-bath! I'm so glad I'm back home!"

When she laughs like she's doing, no one else can laugh.

You can see the teenaged girl inside her face like a skull in an X-ray, can see her those times when Daddy and her would get into it. Like that one time she tried to convince Mom to call the police. She was about to do it, too, but Dad came in from the back room where he used to fix radios and TVs as a sideline to his local radio career, and he said he heard all Lisa's trash talk, and he was goddamn sick of it.

Mom said, "Yes, Lisa, it's trash." She put the phone down.

I was nine then, hiding behind the couch. Marty was home, fourteen, with long hair. He was smoking in the kitchen and had the radio on. Lisa was sixteen. We'd had tacos for dinner, and I remember how many Dad ate: seven. No, eight.

"It's trash, and I'm tired of it," Dad said. He was trying to use his friendly radio voice.

Marty got up. I was peeking from over the couch and he saw me and he said, "Let's go."

I nodded my head no.

"Come on, Phil," Marty said.

Mom and Lisa and Dad got into it big time. I didn't budge. Marty just shrugged. He had a paper sack of clothes, and he took off. He called about three days later saying he was staying with his friend in Bristol, and soon he came home with his hair buzz cut, telling us that he got born again.

Lisa said right back to Dad that night, "How can you do it?" Then she turned around and said to Mom, "How can you let him do it?"

Mom shook her head, like it was too easy to think that way. To think that anybody could stop anything. Dad and Mom were also just sick of her mouth. I was too. I wanted it not to be real, and Lisa wanted it to be everything. There were times when we as a family got along, by the way. Birthdays sometimes. Going to the movies in Johnson City. Sometimes. But Lisa would get crazy and bring it up. She was the only one.

At times, in fact, I felt like a hero, being so shut-mouthed. But not Lisa. That night she grabbed a knife out of a drawer and instead of stabbing Dad cut her own wrist. It looked really stupid the way she did it. I lost respect for her, despite the fact she was trying to save my life. I just crawled out from behind the couch and went outside and climbed a tree.

5

Daddy died a horrible death anyway: diabetes and high blood pressure and finally organ failure. He got gangrene and his foot never healed. He did not obey doctors, ate whatever he wanted, sent Mom out to get Reese's Cups and whole milk and peppermint ice cream and biscuit-sausage sandwiches from the little place over the hill. But his hair always was perfect. He limped around the house on his bad foot, too sick and too tired even to do his part-time radio show, leaving little bloody foot prints all over the floor that Mom cleaned with paper towels.

I never moved away. Dad stopped all the sex stuff when I was a freshman in high school, when he had the nervous breakdown. That was the day Marty graduated from high school.

Caught up in the moment, Dad admitted to Marty he loved him *that* way, more than just a son. He spoke like he was asking his own son for his hand in marriage, like Marty graduating meant it was time to speak of things aloud. Marty was in his black cap and gown. We were all in the living room, getting ready to go.

Lisa by this time had abandoned us, on her way to three husbands and psychotic episodes in other states and a porn movie (maybe) and all that stuff she'd tell me and Mom about in her irregular phone-ins.

Marty smiled at Dad, after Dad whispered his confession. I always imagine it as, "I love you so much, son. Let's run away tonight. Just go and live together way far off in a log cabin. Me and you."

Marty heard what he heard, and then he said back, real loud: "I hope you die a horrible death. I hope you are in so much pain when you die that you regret you ever lived. And then I hope you burn in hell for eternity."

Marty smiled again and walked out in his cap and gown. Eventually he got a job at a gas station and rented his own apartment, and now he's married with two or three kids somewhere, working at a tool factory, making pretty good money. I've heard.

It looked like Dad had lost fifty pounds in one second, in his dark suit, his domed hair shiny as a door knob in a dream.

I felt sorry for him. He collapsed on the floor, in the perfect position to be kicked and burned alive. Sobbing, actually shocked that Marty would hate him.

Mom went to him, held onto him.

Dad wound up in the Johnson City Memorial Hospital, in the psych unit. He was there for three weeks. He admitted everything, apologizing to me in letters I won't ever read again because I ripped them up. The therapy sessions with me and Mom went on and on.

At one of them, Dad said to me, gaunt and in his pajamas and plaid bathrobe, "Your grandpa was an evil man. He whipped me with an electrical cord and he burned my fingers on the stove if I didn't get up in time to do my chores before school. He'd leave without telling me and be gone for days. We were mismatched, me and him, and he tortured me because we were so mismatched. I never learned what love is. Good clean decent love."

Dad smiled telling me all that. All his self-pity made him very happy with himself, and I was glad. In fact, he was crazy-happy, like he'd just discovered some beautiful nugget of gold in the bottom of the commode.

"You see?" he kept saying. This grin made the room shrink to the size of a drawer, and I felt close to him and I wanted him to die. But I loved him too. "You see? That's the kind of stuff that makes people sick like me."

6

Now Mom and me are in the doctor's office that adjoins the examining rooms, beige and maroon wallpaper, files piled up, fluorescent lights buzzing, dusty jelly beans in a candy-dish.

"I don't know," the doctor says, a bald fat man with kind, watery eyes. "I know I told you it was fifty-fifty, but really the odds were pretty much against you, to tell you the truth. But you're biopsy's come back and nothing. We'll still do another chemo in a month, just to do a scorched-earth kind of thing. But, my dear, you're as cancer free as they come."

Mom is in the outfit I like. The navy-blue pantsuit from Sears. She is crying a little. Balled-up Kleenex, the hair she washed pulled back with bobby pins. I smile over at her. She smiles back, confused. She seems to have lost the connection between how she actually feels inside and the real world, but so have I, I guess. About the only real emotions the two of us have left are gratitude and that numb sensation you get when you're opening bills.

"It really might be a miracle," the doctor says, laughing at himself for saying such a thing.

Mom and me go out for soft-serve ice cream to celebrate, but then we remember Lisa is back at home still.

"Don't tell her nothing," Mom says.

"But it's good news."

"Doesn't matter. She's come home after all those years, and she wants it all to be about her."

I look at the ice cream cone that Mom has half-eaten. It is now in the shape caused by her tongue, a white cold little wing.

7

At one time, Mom and Dad and me tried to open our own video-rental and repair shop downtown. Where the day-old-bread store used to be, next to the courthouse. Even back then, there wasn't much business downtown, but we were optimistic. We had some money saved away. It was a small

From Me to You

space. Dad and me made the shelves and a countertop from pinewood and we painted them neon 1984 colors.

By then, Dad had accumulated a thousand-plus videotape-movie collection. He cataloged each video in his spare time, two or three recipe boxes full. He really was a genius in many ways. Everybody at the RadioShack knew him by his first name. People drove miles for him to fix their radios and TVs.

The video place was great for about two weeks. We called it VIDEO PLUS. Dad got free advertising on his radio show. We had posters on the wall of *Splash* and *Ghostbusters*, and we had a cardboard cutout of the thing from *Alien*. Mom ran the register and kept the books.

For two weeks we were Anita, Wayne and Phil Keesling, video-rental and repair shop owners. A family running a business. But then the business stopped almost like a head getting chopped off.

The last day, we had a pizza party. Just the three of us. Dad was having health problems, but we didn't know why. The pizza was the deep dish he so much loved. We had boxed up the last video and taken down the last movie poster.

I was twenty-five years old, still living at home, spending most of my time thinking of how not to do or be anything. Finding pleasure in the secrecy of what had been done to me, and also how I had survived. I knew that I would eventually disappear that way.

I remember Dad looking prouder that day than he'd ever been while running the place, like he felt more comfortable in the twilight of his work, when there was no possibility of hope.

I realize now that the hope came from knowing there was nothing left, that you had given your all and that still wasn't enough.

Dad said that last day in VIDEO PLUS, wiping his hand on a napkin, "Don't let this discourage you." He was looking right at me. "We got to keep on trying, don't we?"

"I guess," I said.

8

Dean and Lisa have decorated the house in our absence. This is what must have been on Lisa's list: balloons and pop and streamers and ham-salad sandwiches and chips and a big cake that says HAPPY BIRTHDAY EVERYBODY ON EARTH!!! Even a piñata.

Lisa is a little hysterical.

"Well, this is nice," Mom says.

Dean says, "She's always doing something like this." He doesn't make eye contact. "Making up reasons for parties. She even made me get her a karaoke machine."

There it is, on the table next to the La-Z-Boy, where Dad used to keep his reel-to-reel tape machine and stereo. A speaker and a microphone on a stand. Lisa is in a red nightgown that is too tight on her.

"This is what I call a party for nothing," she says, laughing. "You have a great big party just because you want to!"

She goes over to the karaoke machine and turns it on. Music comes out. Dean gets the lights. The curtains have already been pulled closed. Dean lights candles on the table. Lisa is in an amber glow.

The song is by Olivia Newton-John. It is called "Have You Ever Been Mellow?" Lisa sings along with the voice on the speaker. She knows it by heart. Her voice is low-pitched, and it fills the room: *Have you ever been mellow? Have you ever triiied? Have you ever had someone to love?*

We eat cake and we smile and we listen to her.

At one point Lisa comes over to me between her songs and says into the microphone, "God loves you, you poor thing."

Her breath is like rotten peaches, and her face is melting off onto the floor. She wants so bad to be beautiful like in those pictures—the ones that pharmacist guy took of her in his basement studio when she was seventeen, her in a white gown in front of a Hawaiian waterfall, her in a black dress standing next to a stuffed panther, her in a halter top and short shorts next to a bale of hay. She wanted to be a model/actress in Florida but she had a child-molester dad and a house made of plywood in her head. Plus the pharmacist turned out to be a big drug addict himself.

She gets up from kissing my forehead and Mom smiles over at me.

Lisa says, "Do the piñata now." She's still talking into the microphone.

"Lisa likes to have fun," Dean whispers.

"Where did you find a piñata in East Tennessee, Dean?" Mom asks.

"Target."

It's a papier-mâché pig with green eyes, hung from the ceiling by a nail and yarn. Dean puts a blindfold over my eyes, gives me a stick. He leads me to the piñata, and he whispers, "You okay?"

"Yeah."

"Spin him around, Dean!" Lisa says into the microphone. "Make him real dizzy." She laughs and starts to cough.

"You mind?" Dean says.

"No."

Dean spins me around and around, and I swing at the pig and miss, but then finally I pound it and knock it down. Inside are tiny pieces of cheap candy and bubblegum and little toys.

Lisa says into the microphone, "It's all yours, kiddo. Everything inside that thing is yours, honey. From me to you, baby."

Then she starts singing again. Dean adjusts the sound.

I go over to Mom and whisper into her ear.

"I'm so glad you don't have cancer anymore."

Mom nods her head toward Lisa, shushing me.

"Let her sing," Mom whispers back.

9

The next morning, Dean knocks on my door.

"Lisa's dead," he says through the wood.

This is my bedroom: big and cluttered and full of library books and video-tapes and equipment I buy at flea markets. I get up and I don't feel anything. Down the hall is her old bedroom, with peach walls still and that same mirror covered in lipstick that could not be wiped off. She's in her bed, sunken down deep like the bed has swallowed her, a bottle of whatever on the floor.

You can tell Dean does not like to cry, but here he is doing just that. I don't cry. This is why she came back. This is why Grandpa Zero built the house, I'm thinking: just for her, a good place to collapse all the way in that puddle of sheets.

I take the covers all the way off of Lisa. She's naked and pale and big like a cloud in a box.

I reach down and feel around her neck. I know this feeling. It's the one that explodes about five hours after the body's been removed, when you're alone and there's the funeral. I have to tell Mom. I will have to call Marty who will not come to the funeral as he has wiped this house clean out of mind, burned it down about sixty thousand times.

"We fell asleep together," Dean says, crying still and explaining, like a little kid in trouble.

The room has shadows all over it. I look at Lisa, and I think I should cover her back up. So I do.

"We fell asleep together and I thought she was asleep but she wasn't. She was dead," Dean says. "I thought we were just, you know, holding onto one another, sleeping, but she was dead."

10

When Dad was about to die, he propped himself up in that back room where he used to fix the TVs and other equipment. A naked window's glass was busted out and taped over. Dad was trying his hand at rehabbing an old computer with the tiniest tools and a pegboard wall filled with different colors of wire. His leg stump was attached to a drain-off bag. He had to be carried in and out. I was the carrier.

Dad yelled for me one morning. I walked in. He was on his work stool, staring out the window at two heavyset men we had hired to dig a new septic tank. The one Grandpa Zero had put in leaked real bad. I stood beside Dad. He and I looked out at the men digging. Surrounded by autumn mountains, they were using shovels, having plowed out the vicinity with a dozer. It was sunny and chilly. They were faceless.

"How much are they charging us, Phil?" Dad asked.

I was making sure his drain-off bag was secured so it wouldn't fall off and bust.

"I don't know. Mom worked it out."

"I bet it's a pretty penny."

"I don't know."

He said he might take himself a little nap. I tried to pick him up, but he pushed me away for a second. I had got my job at the library by then—cleaning off the acetate-covered books with ammonia and water, shelving them carefully, during the quiet time, the only time that matters.

Dad wanted to watch them dig for a second. It was like they were digging for some kind of treasure they were going to end up giving him. I wondered why we were still living together, me and him, but I knew. I watched them dig too. The shovels made music like hands beating on walls.

"You know why I'm not a monster?" Dad said eventually. His eyes were still looking out that window.

I didn't say anything.

"It's because I never ran away."

I said, "Oh."

"I stayed, didn't I? I stayed with my family. That's why I'm not a monster."

I picked him up and carried him to the wheelchair I had found in a yard sale, making sure the drain-off bag was okay. He looked at me as I got him into the chair. He was smiling, but you could tell the pain was eating at him.

"You love me don't you?"

I said yes.

Queers Can't Hear

I

Leon is all over me at my place. It's cloudy October outside the halfway-pulled curtains. Only power lines and the sawed-off-shotgun-looking tree-tops are visible. I live in a studio apartment above a Christian bookstore.

Me and Leon do it on the couch. After we get our pants back on, he goes to the bathroom and comes back out, pulls a bottle of pop out of his jacket pocket.

"You ever try Pepsi Edge?" He shows off the bottle.

I turn on the CD player and say nothing.

Leon's hair is dyed black and he has sideburns that connect to his mustache. One time I asked him if he got the joke—you know, his Wolverine facial hair and all—and he said, "Of course." But he likes the way it looks.

"Pepsi Edge. Fifty percent less carbs, but one hundred percent taste," he goes, laughing and standing there, licking his lips. He twists off the lid.

"No, I have never tried Pepsi fucking Edge." I laugh too.

Leon comes over and gives me one of his sloppy kisses. He's always talking about stupid shit because there's no way we are going to talk about anything that's actually going on.

"Patty is probably scared," he whispers.

"Yeah," I say.

Patty is Leon's ex-wife. She's also the mother of Donny, who's been my best friend since first grade. Even though they got a divorce, Leon still lives with Patty. She had a stroke about six years back, when she was thirty-nine. Now she has that left-arm thing and her face is in a perpetual lop-slide. She doesn't go out much.

"Hey, I know." Leon's still whispering. "I'll get her some Pepsi Edge." He smiles, kind of sad.

I'm never really sure why I do what I do with Leon, but right then I can see in his small squirrelly eyes some deep feeling working its way out, a real pitch-black sadness, not just about Patty and me and Donny, but about everything in the whole world. That's what does it, I guess, what makes me always kiss him back and everything else.

"Hey, Leon?" I ask, standing there in my apartment shirtless, skin and bones with a shaved head.

"What?" He backs up against the door. Another swig until it's almost gone.

"Say Pepsi Edge one more time for me."

He whispers, real sexy with closed eyes, smiling without showing any teeth: "Pepsi Edge. Pepsi Edge. Pepsi Edge."

2

Donny and me are at his place in a trailer park behind the chili place. We can play loud music because Donny's trailer is way in the back. We're sitting outside on lawn chairs. It's kind of chilly but nice and we've got beer and a bag of sour cream and onion potato chips I picked up from the convenience store on my way over after work. And yes, work sucked tonight. I do telemarketing bull-shit for Daytech, Inc.

"We ever finish 'Blackbelt'?" Donny goes, all cavalier and sounding tired of everything. He lights up a Marlboro Menthol.

"Blackbelt" is one of our songs. Donny and me are two thirds of Noxious Waste, a band we got going in high school seven years back. I play drums, Donny guitar, and this other guy, Trey, he's got bass. It's kind of amazing we're still at it. But by now it's just a thing we do to get over everything else we have to do.

"I think it's ready for its debut," I go. I'm trying to sound hopeful. We got a gig at Squeezer's (over on Cloverdale Avenue, across the street from Donato's) next week, Halloween weekend.

Donny is the opposite of his dad. He's got a blonde crewcut and a goatee. He's not so tan and has eyes that look like a cartoon of ice melting. But they share the same kind of nervous attitude. Donny and me used to do it when we were in high school. Hell, I even used to make believe we were boyfriends. It was only playing around for him, though, and he outgrew it and we've never said one word about it since.

"I guess we need to practice." Donny rolls his eyes like it is just one more thing on his crazy, crazy to-do list. Gets his cell phone out, calls Trey, who is at Don Pablo's washing dishes.

"No, man. Tonight. You're not tired. Take a magnum. I'll make a pot of coffee. Okay? Tonight." He flicks off the phone.

"He'll be off in an hour," Donny says, pocketing his cell phone.

He starts talking about his janitorial service idea, how he has the papers to incorporate it. He's going to run an ad on the internet so that he can "target" small-business people. All that business-targeting crap is from his fiancée, Sarah. She goes to community college in Middletown.

"Yeah, it'll be great, you know, having my own business. Being my own boss. Making my own rules." The light over his trailer's busted-up screen door makes his eye sockets look empty.

I just nod my head and say, "I'm freezing."

We go in. I get settled in behind my drum set, which is black vinyl and silver. It was purchased for me by my now deceased grandma from Kentucky. Donny nukes his leftover burrito. While he eats it, I sit there and think about when I had a car. This was when Donny was living with Leon and Patty, a year or so ago. I was over at their place. Me and Donny had watched some DVDs, and he got so ripped he just passed out. Of course Patty was hiding.

My car stalled out on me and Leon tried to fix it, but he only made things worse.

Motherfucker takes the carburetor out, when the problem is just that I don't have a gas cap and water has got into the gas tank. Once he takes the carburetor out and starts fooling with it, though, my Dodge Neon is a lost cause.

We go into the kitchen, this little yellow apartment kitchen. There's Leon with his sideburns and his reddish tan and his muscular arms, looking down at the carburetor like it's some tiny animal he's operating on. Then he looks up at me. He's always known, and I have too, and he says: "Come here."

Out in the dark living room, the A-C is humming. I'm a little drunk, thinking of the carburetor in there on a blue bath towel on top of the kitchen table, a heart with oily screws and other parts taken out of it. Leon kisses me on the mouth. Our teeth knock into each other. We do it quiet and quick. I mean, when I was growing up he was this big joke between me and Donny—Mr. Sideburns, Mr. Ask-Too-Many-Fucking-Questions, Mr. Crying-in-the-Living-Room-with-a-Sad-Movie-on. He never tried nothing with me when I was a kid, but I could tell right then he'd wanted to do this a long time. And funny thing: I did not mind.

Now Donny wipes his mouth with a paper towel.

"Dad's been a real asshole lately," he says, looking at the wall, wadding the paper towel up and throwing it down the hall. "Like today he was supposed to take Mom to the foot doctor but he didn't show up and Mom didn't know where he was. So she calls me and I don't understand a thing she's saying."

"Yeah."

I smile, real stupid looking, I'm sure.

"I mean, okay, they're divorced, but he's the one that's decided to stay there with her, you know?"

Donny straps on his guitar, fidgets with it, goes silent. He doesn't know that me and his dad are doing it. No way. If somebody were to tell him, he'd want to bash that person's brains in, and then come after me and Leon, not necessarily in that order. I mean, he doesn't bash people's brains in, he's a skinny little fuck like me, so maybe he'd get a gun or something. But still Donny'd be so pissed he would not let me sit here in his trailer like this. Donny strokes his guitar, and the sound is like comical little knives killing comical little people. Across the room, electrical-taped to a paneled wall, is one of the Xeroxes we've been staple-gunning to telephone poles: NOXIOUS WASTE, PUNK

OUT FEST @ SQUEEZER'S *Friday and Saturday May 9 and 10—just two dollar cover!!!* with one of Donny's fucked-up snake cartoons—a boa, with an eye-patch and a dirty-looking mustache, wrapped around a bulging arm.

Trey shows up, wet and tired.

"Who hates life, everybody raise their hands," he goes, taking off his Don Pablo shirt. Buzz cut too, with a tattoo on his shoulder, Princess Amidala.

I start the festivities with "Blackbelt," which I wrote in fifteen minutes, to be honest. Donny had a kind of Alice-in-Chains riff and I just got the words going and then Trey came in with the undertones. All our songs are about three minutes long and, even though it's just us three, we make a lot of noise.

Here are the lyrics I wrote: "Blackbelt motherfucker/got no place to go/ blackbelt motherfucker/takes it nice and slow/blackbelt stupid fucker/always wants to know/blackbelt stupid fucker/asshole has to go!"

We do "Blackbelt" four times, then renditions of "There's No Telling Why" and "Lay Off" and "Bliss Piss."

It's almost 3:00 in the morning when I get my coat. Trey yawns. My ears are totally shot. Donny says something to me.

"What?"

He yells, a big asshole grin on his face: "I said 'queers can't hear!'"

That was a joke from high school, back in the day. Some dumb fuck would come up to you in line in the cafeteria or in gym and pantomime talking, and then you go, "What?" and the dude goes, "Queers can't hear!"

I laugh and Donny keeps on looking at me, the grin dropping from his face. "Bye," he goes, now using this weird fake deep voice.

"What?"

"I'm just tired," Donny says back.

Trey is on the floor now, completely crashed. Donny comes over while I zip up my coat. His breath smells kind of bad from cigarettes and the burrito and being tired. He looks me in the eye right when I look up after zipping my coat up.

"So, I got a question for you," he says.

"Yeah?"

"When the fuck are we gonna grow up?" He's smiling, dark circles under his eyes. "I mean, when are all of us, you know, gonna fucking grow up?"

Those words at 3:00 in the morning, right after we played like crap, and him looking so sure of our suckiness, that's just fucking great.

"I'm grown up," I say.

"Never mind, go on," Donny says. Then suddenly he's laughing real loud.

"Man, I'm one of the walking dead," I say, laughing too.

I'm out of there. I start walking the ten blocks home. It's cold as fuck now. The neighborhood is all old shacks with toys and kitchen chairs on the porches. The sidewalks are lopsided. I arrive at the Heavenly Garden, the Christian bookstore I live above. A yellow and blue cross is painted on the plate-glass display window. There's an amber security light glowing on all the religious crap inside: a cardboard cutout of some gospel singer, a shelf of felt cutout bible-story people, racks of Christian CDs. I stand there for a sec, then go behind, to the black wrought-iron fire-escape steps that take me to the door to my place upstairs. But I just can't make myself go up. I can see my shitty little apartment in my head, lit by that one lamp that doesn't have a shade.

I go over to Leon's, two blocks down. When I knock I feel like I'm gonna be in big trouble. But that's what's making me knock, that feeling.

Leon comes to the door.

"Can't sleep," I whisper.

"Come on in," he says. He does that thing where he bites his thumbnail, looking at me.

He sits down on a black La-Z-Boy, and I can hear Patty snoring in the next room. I flop down on the couch like some stupid twerp. Leon gets up from the Boy and sits on the couch. He looks at me like I am the answer to all his prayers, this happiness spilling out of his eyes and face like a blast of heat. We are completely silent. He gets down on the floor in front of me, his knees cracking. I unzip my jeans. He pulls them off me real slow, and for a minute it looks like he is sixteen years old or something, like when we do this the young sweet part of him gets let out. He kisses my thighs real soft.

After it's over, he gets up and thinks he hears Patty, but it's just the furnace kicking on.

Then Leon kisses my forehead and kind of laughs under his breath and, without another word, goes to bed.

I'm half asleep when I hear Patty get up, an hour or so later. I have a good view of the kitchen. She's short and pale, like the bottom of a plastic milk carton, with ratty blonde hair. Her left arm swings slowly by her side. She's got one big eye and one little one. She opens a cabinet door real slow, gets out a bowl and a box of instant oatmeal.

Patty rips open the envelope of instant oatmeal after struggling with the box. I watch her feet drag on the linoleum as she goes to open the microwave door. She puts in the bowl, slams the door, then has a little trouble pressing buttons. But the microwave goes on and she waits. Once the oatmeal is done, she drags herself over to a chair at the yellow table and practically collapses into it.

She spoons the gray instant oatmeal into her mouth. It's another victory for her, you might could say. She doesn't even know there's somebody crashing on her couch and eyeing her. She just gets her breakfast and starts her day like any other. All alone in her goddamn stupid kitchen.

3

I quit Daytech five days after getting the job. I was on the phone trying to do some survey about vacuum cleaners and this guy said that I should be ashamed of myself calling him at home. I said sir, this is my job and he said get another one and then he went on to say while you're at it, get a life too.

I was in a closed-down, gutted Walgreens with about twenty other losers, sitting at an old gray metal desk, wearing a headset connected to a computer. The dude's words just made way too much sense. I got up and told the lady manager I was going out for a smoke break, and I just walked back to my apartment and changed and went over to Donny's.

Me and Donny and Trey try to practice again but we sound shitty and Trey has to go to work anyway. On the way to take Trey to work, I tell them about quitting my job and they just nod their heads, probably thinking "par for the course."

And Trey goes, "I can get you on at Don Pablo's."

I get an application and fold it and put it in my back pocket. Eventually it will magically turn into a bunch of white fluffy shit in a laundromat dryer.

Donny and me go back to his trailer and hang out mostly in silence, but then Sarah shows up in her mom's minivan. She and Donny are going out to eat somewhere. I am not invited.

Sarah is taller than Donny and a little overweight, with brown hair cut short. She's always lighting up a cigarette, chewing gum, looking at her freshly painted fingernails to see if they're still freshly painted, I guess. Donny's dressed in a button-down shirt and nice pants and black shoes. She's in a sky-blue skirt thing, with high heels. I'm setting at my drum set, inhaling their secondhand smoke.

"I'm real sorry," Sarah says to me after Donny tells her I quit my job.

"It was just monotonous, you know?" I say without making eye contact.

"Yeah, I know. Maybe we'll be able to hire you once we get the janitor service up and running." She chomps on her gum and smiles at me like I matter to her in a certain small way she hasn't discovered as of yet but she is really trying hard to figure it all out.

Donny and her met online when he had a computer, before he pawned it. She's six years older and has a kid that she let get adopted by her ex-husband and his new wife. Now she is career-oriented. That's what she tells people. She's going to community college to be a paralegal or some shit.

Donny smells like cologne. Teeth brushed, hair combed back. I pretend-drum. But I see him, and I think about how when we first started up the band it was kind of like we were married when we played together. We practiced day and night in my stepdad's garage or wherever we could find, and the music made us feel like birds flying into clouds made of chainsaws. It wasn't the greatest music, okay, I know that. Probably some people would not even call it music. But we did, and we pretended we were great, and that's kind of like love, isn't it?

"So you guys have a Halloween gig at Squeezer's?" Sarah says, after kissing Donny in a real showoff way.

She's helping with the janitorial thing all the time now—scheduling appointments, making initial phone-calls, doing other public-relations activities. She says her dad, who works for the county, may front part of the start-up money they need to purchase a really good industrial vacuum cleaner and blah blah blah.

"Yeah. Halloween night," Donny says.

"Halloween night," I repeat like an idiot.

"That'll be fun," Sarah goes. "Halloween at Squeezer's with Noxious Waste!" She yells that part. Then she does the thing where she jumps up and down saying Noxious Waste over and over, like she is trying to improve our spirits. Or maybe she's just putting us down.

Donny laughs. I look at my sticks tapping the drums. Then she stops. I look up and Donny and Sarah are gone.

Me and Leon hook up that evening and go get vodka tonics at this gay bar in Cincinnati close to the river. It's maybe 1:00 AM, crowded. Leon in a plaid shirt and real tight jeans and sandals in October. Sandals with dark socks. His face is skeletal in the disco lights, his sideburns like hairy little arms hugging the sides of his face. All around us are shirtless muscle freaks, hungry-eyed nobodies, giggling girls slumming it for fun. Smells like a sewer of cologne and cigarettes and sweat. The music is tripped-out versions of Elton John and Madonna and that one "Gloria" song. Just pure shit. I drink too much and Leon drinks more than that, and then he says something I can't hear.

"What?"

He laughs.

"I think Donny knows," he yells. Fucker is smiling!

I wonder to myself why he saved that little tidbit for tonight here in the gay bar. It's because he's screwed up. He is pure white-trash pervert material and, oh yeah, I hate his fucking guts.

I make him go outside to the back of the place where it's a little quieter. People are coming in and out, but the music isn't so obnoxious. We go past the paved parking lot to the part covered in gravel.

"What did Donny say?" I ask, standing near some weeds.

"I don't know. I mean, I just got the feeling when I was talking to him on the phone. He cussed me out about not taking Patty to her foot doctor appointment last week, and then he asks me where I was, real intense."

"Damn," I say, totally pissed at him for terrifying me. "That doesn't mean anything."

Leon is so damn drunk. It's cold. He's shaky and he has the saddest eyes right then. Eyes like little puncture holes in a cardboard box for some animal that's already died inside it. But then he smiles, and I get pissed. I guess I knock him down. He falls hard. I mean drunk-assed hard. Like head-first, and for a second or two he just lies there, and I'm standing over him. He finally gets up. His forehead is scraped good, rocks embedded in his skin. His eyelids and nose are all blood-covered.

Leon just grins. Then he starts walking to his car, which is pretty close. We pass some other people going into the bar, but no one stops to check or anything. We get in the car. I drive, and I guess I'm supposed to tell him things. But all I can do right then is look at his bloody forehead in the passing headlights while he just sits there.

Leon starts to cry. I mean big-time cry. I feel like I know him for everything he is when I see him do that. I know how he has to get up every morning and look at himself and say, *It's okay, it's cool, simmer down my friend, everything is going to work out just fine, just pull it together mofo.* I know how he takes everything so serious, to the point that he does outlandish shit like divorce his stroke-victim wife and then still stay with her and take care of her and help her take baths and go grocery-shopping for her because she's afraid of leaving her house.

I pull into an all-night hamburger place, run in and get some napkins. He puts a couple on his face. He stops the crying. I park in front of his apartment building. After I give him his car keys back, he gets out and walks away without one word.

I go, "Leon?"

He just keeps on walking up to the glass doors in the front of his building, and I follow. He walks in, shuts the door, turns and looks at me through the glass. Under the fluorescent lights inside there are metal mailboxes and a big fake houseplant and an empty bulletin-board. He stands with both his hands on the door handle. Then he says something. I try to open the door, but he holds it closed.

I say, "What?"

He has that broken face. Napkins and blood. The sideburns, the eyes.

"This is not me," he says through the glass door. "Not me."

He turns around real slow and walks up the stairs.

4

One of the conditions of my cheap-shit rent—I mean, I only pay a hundred a month—is that on Sunday mornings I have to go to Faith United Baptist on Thornberry Road with Bev and Karl Dunkirk, the owners of Heavenly Garden. Karl's got a low-pitched radio-deejay voice, and Bev's loud and flighty and way bigger than him. They make a pretty killer team on Sunday mornings: him all short with a silver goatee in jeans and a dress shirt, and her all tall with perminated hair shiny as tinsel.

Me and Bev and Karl even sit together, like a family or something. I don't have any family left in the area. My dad's in rehab up in Terre Haute, where his morbidly obese girlfriend lives, and my mom is in Louisville with her, like, forty-ninth husband.

Today I'm dressed in a maroon sweater and khakis, the outfit I always wear. The auditorium at Faith United Baptist has mint-green cinderblock walls and a baptismal pool with dusty stage curtains behind it. The pews are dark plastic. The skinny minister preaches about how the world is going to hell. And I'm thinking, you said it brother. I look around and seventy percent of the congregation is completely fat and depressed, and church really helps them, I'd say. Or maybe not. They smile like, now that they're here, they have something to live for. But only in this place and at this exact moment.

Bev and Karl drive me over to Donny's after church. We're going to practice again. Karl drives a huge powder-blue Impala, like a chariot. Bev turns around in the front seat and faces me. I try to look like a Christian so they won't evict me.

"Pretty nice sermon, huh?" she says and smiles.

Karl brakes at a stoplight: "You ever think about going up when the preacher asks about getting born again, Matt?"

He's looking at me in the rearview mirror, like he is trying to figure me out, trying to see which little slot in his head I fit into.

"Yeah, I think about it," I say, and I feel like I might cry, flashing on Leon in tears last night. Dumbass falling headfirst to the ground, kind of like Lucifer when he got kicked out of heaven.

"We're glad you go to church with us, kiddo," Bev says as Karl speeds off. "I mean, you know you don't have to. We'd charge you the same rent whether you go or not."

I want to say, *Right*—you know, in a real smartass tone. But I don't.

Bev laughs, like it's a big joke, then goes all serious. Judgment comes into her eyes like two great big crows landing on two side-by-side mailboxes. Her bright blonde hair catches the October sunshine like tinfoil.

"We know the truth about you," she says.

"Truth?" I smile.

"You're a punk rocker, and punk rockers normally don't go to church, do they Karl?"

They both laugh.

"No," he says, almost in a mean way. "There's Christian rockers though. We carry a lot of their CDs. The Christian rockers' CDs. Christians can rock."

+

Bev and Karl drop me off at Donny's trailer. I let myself in. No Donny. There's my drum set, but I'm too tired to practice or even fool around. In the kitchen there's an empty box of Cocoa Puffs. Donny's electric guitar is on the floor by a bean bag chair and a bag of garbage. I take the trash out to the dumpster and come back. Then I go to the one bedroom the trailer has and open the door.

Queers Can't Hear

No curtains on the window. Mattress and box spring on the floor, along with comic books and old textbooks from his one semester in college. Notebook or two half-filled. Poster of Stain'd. There's his smell, like old bread and gasoline. Dirty clothes in the corner. Sarah's perfume.

I pick up one of his tee-shirts off the floor and smell it. It is a dream, taking him into my nose, letting him turn into a blue vapor in my head. I remember always letting him know how much he did not mean to me just so he could mean everything to me.

When I collapse onto his bed and start jacking off, it's real stupid and slow. There's music in my head and there's love and there's the secret people like me have, the reason we do what we have to do. I know I'm alive. No guessing or bullshit about it. I am motherfucking here on earth.

5

Halloween night at Squeezer's, everybody!

Some people have taken it upon themselves to dress up like pirates and sluts and Darth Vader, but tonight's not really that different than any other. Me and Trey had to set up the instruments because Donny was at some insurance appointment for his new janitorial bullshit (on a Saturday, right, sure).

Donny's here now, though, checking the amp. Sarah is dressed up like *I Dream of Jeannie*, her belly hanging out, and Donny's dressed like that astronaut dude in the show. I've got on a big old black garbage bag, tied around my neck and filled with newspaper, naked white legs and some black sneakers underneath. Trey is trying to pull off Jeff Gordon, Nascar Super Stud.

It's not that crowded. 9:00 PM. Smells of puke and dropped booze and cigarette smoke. Sarah jumps up and down. She wants to let the cat out of the bag, you can tell, wants to let me know something. Earlier this week, she and Donny started looking for an apartment.

Soon enough we start, with "Blackbelt." Donny clangs the first chords on his guitar, and right when I come in with the backbeat, drumming so hard I can feel my bones coming out of my skin, all the lights in Squeezer's go off completely. No shit. The place goes black. People start screaming and laughing. It's not even storming outside.

Somebody asks if J.R., the guy who owns the place, paid his electric bill. But then someone comes in and says the whole neighborhood is blacked out.

"It's Halloween, man!" a drunk dude screams. People applaud really loud, like what he said was truly meaningful.

Me and Trey and Donny stand there, stunned by this mysterious turn of events: an astronaut, a race-car driver, and a bag of garbage with instruments. We could go acoustic, I guess. I don't know.

Donny unstraps his guitar. I can barely see him. Then someone has a flashlight and the beam catches his face. He looks like he's happy it's finally all over.

The flashlight beam disappears. Donny turns to me.

"Fucking forget this shit," he says.

And just like that, he and Sarah are gone. Me and Trey laugh.

"I guess we're waiting for the power to come back on," Trey says. "I guess we're waiting for all this shit to make sense." He laughs because he's nervous.

I get up from behind the drums, thinking about chasing after Donny. But when I am almost at the front door, the lights come back on, and I see Leon standing beside a table. He has the stupidest-looking Band-Aid job on his face, five or six of them taped willy-nilly over his little wounds like Scotch-tape on a broken mirror.

"I was gonna watch your show," he says.

I just look at him, unable to say anything.

Leon smiles, like nothing has ever happened between us, like this is just the beginning of a fun evening for him.

"Happy Halloween," he says.

Queers Can't Hear

Happy That They Hate Us

Six kids, not one of them lives with us, and here I am, you-know-what again. It's not Cecil's, but that's no big surprise. Once I tell him, he'll look at me like I just shot him, and then he'll go off somewhere and find a way to get the bullet out of his heart with some matches and a kitchen knife.

The guy down at the BP station, he's the father. I would spend time there, eating Starbursts and looking at magazines and sitting behind the counter. He's older and kind of dumb, but not ugly. We did it in his truck out by the dam the Tennessee Valley Authority built way back when. It wasn't great but I knew what I was doing. If you think I wanted to get pregnant, I think I did too. After the fucking, I looked out the back window and saw fog come off the dammed-up water like bedcovers floating in slow motion off a bed in some supernatural demon-possession DVD.

Cecil's mom is a bitch, by the way.

Fat cow's at our trailer, looking through it like we're hiding something important from her. She tries not to be obvious. She's looking for drugs, I bet. Now hear this: *I do not do drugs when I am pregnant.*

"Cecil's granny is doing well," she says, standing near some unwashed clothes and the washer that just backs up water onto the floor.

Cecil's mom is in her Sunday dress even though it's Thursday. Snow's coming down in the windows. Keanu and Liam are out in the minivan she got with the money that was left over after Cecil's granny was packed off to the nursing home. They sold all of the old lady's things, even her little house, so she could go on Medicaid. Now Cecil's mom thinks she's hot shit with the van and the new couch that makes the bed where Keanu and Liam are sleeping.

Keanu and Liam are my boys but Cecil's mom takes care of them, and that's okay with everybody so please don't think nothing. I see them when I want. It's better this way. They don't want me to be that for them and I don't want to be that for them either. We all understand. Sometimes I even feel like me and Liam and Keanu are brothers and sister. I named them though, and those names stuck.

They don't like coming over to the trailer very often.

Cecil's mom says, "Are you eating okay?"

She looks worried.

"Where you going all dressed up?"

"Johnson City. Taking the boys to the dentist, then we're taking momma them peanut-butter cookies she likes." Cecil's mom smiles great big.

"Johnson City? Can I go?" I know what she'll say but I don't care. I see an opportunity and I'm on it: the flea market with the two-dollar DVDs. I'm always looking for DVDs. People from all over my trailer park come to borrow movies from me. My nickname is Blockbuster. I'm Blockbuster for free and I don't mind. Neighbor helping neighbor. I'm obsessed and spend money I don't have on movies we don't need. But then every time I buy a new one, I think to myself how someone else will want to watch it. I'm providing an act of human kindness, so I spend money I don't got.

"I don't know, honey. Don't you got things to do?" Cecil's mom says, all serious and mean looking, scanning the trailer again like it's the scene of some horrendous crime.

I nod but then go into the bedroom and get on my jeans—which hardly fit, I'm almost two months now—and put on my boots and my big coat. Yes, I told Cecil's mom I was pregnant before telling Cecil, told her right after church last week while we were waiting in the drive-through line at a chicken place. I was trying to act all innocent and stupid, maybe even a little bit tragic, trying to let her know that what had happened was not my fault. But of course in the back seat were Liam and Keanu, proof of what I am. There's four other ones of mine out there, all adopted into good homes, I guess, all named by me but renamed by the people that took them. "Took with permission," I mean. Nothing sinister.

Winter sunshine and the smell of fried chicken and Cecil's mom's perfume mixed together. Liam and Keanu were in jeans and nice shirts and new shoes and new coats. Keanu was nine years old and too skinny. Lately he'd been dressing up like Osama bin Laden in the basement for some imaginary movie he was making with a broken video camera. Liam was seven and sucked his thumb.

As she pulled up to the window, I said, "I'm pregnant again, Mrs. Blevins." I called her "Mrs. Blevins" when we were on good terms.

"Oh no," she says.

Keanu jumped up from the back seat and got right into my face. "Why don't you get an abortion?"

Nine years old!

Cecil's mom slapped him back into the seat and she didn't say a word to him except, "One."

"Abortion!" Keanu yelled.

"Two," Cecil's mom counted, paying the skinny guy for the bucket of chicken, which she gave to me to hold on my lap.

"Abort the little fucker!" says Keanu.

"Three," Cecil's mom said.

She parked the minivan and pulled Keanu out of the backseat and spanked him while me and Liam waited. The chicken smelled so good. Liam told me to turn the radio on. His voice was like a little mouse's.

"She's got the keys, honey," I said.

"It's getting cold in here," he said.

Happy That They Hate Us

"I know."

When Cecil's mom was finished, she grabbed Keanu, shoved him back into the van and got into the front seat. She turned toward me, red-faced from the domestic violence she just did in the parking lot.

"Lord God, girl," she said, and it was a whisper like you might whisper at a baby. Her eyes were filled with real tears.

"I'm sorry," I said, and I burst into tears too. I wiped my eyes with the back of my arm, and I tried to look away.

But Cecil's mom goes, "We'll have to get you those vitamins you had last time."

I got choked on crying but then said, "Okay."

She almost got hit pulling out, and Keanu says from the backseat, his butt probably still stinging: "Way to go, fat ass."

+

We take Liam and Keanu to the dentist but then find out the dentist doesn't take Medicaid any more. At one time he did but now he doesn't because of the paperwork, the lady at the front desk said. Keanu and Liam are excited that they don't have to get their teeth done. I'm excited too about you-know-what. Something inside me is calling out to DVDs that I don't really care about and want to own just because maybe somebody else will want to see them. I mean, I don't care really what the movie is as long as I can buy it cheap and take it home and put it in alphabetical order with the others. I even write down the name and the year it was made in a little notebook. I guess this makes me feel civilized.

I watch every one, though, so I know what I've bought. Like last week a Hollywood Video was closing in Kingsport and I bought twenty movies for one dollar apiece and then watched them over three days: *Alien vs. Predator, Angels in the Outfield, Assassins, Blues Brothers 2000, Born on the Fourth of July, Bad Boys 2, California Suite, Casino, Enough, Gorillas in the Mist, Heart Like a Wheel, Jarhead, The Killing Fields, The Matrix Revolutions, Meatballs, Mission: Impossible III, Scream 3, Superman II, Syriana,* and *You've Got Mail.*

By the end of it I was in a dream of ghosts and monsters and skies and people trying hard to be decent and galaxies exploding and guns going off, until all sense was lost. I was pregnant, pregnant like I wanted to be, and each movie fed into the other real bad; it was like they were being crocheted together with my pregnancy in my mind. Cecil would come through, getting ready for work or eating cereal or getting home from work, and I would just sit, not really enjoying the movies as much as owning them with my eyes.

The same feeling comes up on me at the Hoyt and Lester Flea Market Emporium by the interstate in Johnson City, which is where we go after the dentist. I was able to talk Cecil's mom into stopping there before we go to Cecil's granny's nursing home. Cecil's mom has a motive too: she likes to look through the antique lamps and the big sweatpants in different colors. The boys like it because they can get a cheap toy. One each. I even said I would chip in with Cecil's mom on the toys, but she said she could afford them.

It's not too busy at the Hoyt and Lester Flea Market Emporium because it's a winter work-day. Only a few of the booths inside the big warehouse building have sellers in them. But thank God there's one that has DVDs for sale, in big bins I go through like I am searching for gold. It feels like that sometimes, trying to find DVDs I don't got as of yet. My collection has two hundred and twenty-three titles in it right now.

I hear Cecil's mom yell at Liam and Keanu a ways away, and the whole atmosphere gets filled up with her voice while my eyes roam over pictures of Goldie Hawn and Julia Roberts and Keanu Reeves (who, yes, my son is named after) and Chuck Norris. The sign says "five dollars each," but I take five movies I don't have and go over to the guy sitting on a folding chair. Big belly and little head. I am about to ask him if I can have them for half price (because that's what you do at a flea market) when suddenly I feel like my stomach might drop out from between my legs. My face drains out of itself and blood seeps down into my fingertips and it's like I'm riding on an airplane without any heat. I just drop the damn movies and find a bathroom quick, and then, like that, Baby Number Seven is gone. A bloody little nothing.

I look at it down in the commode for about a second, feeling lost and all alone in the flea market bathroom, feeling like an alkie whose bottle's done, who doesn't have the money or the energy to get more booze, who's just stuck with herself. Which is what I am in this lavender-painted stall that has a Christmas wreath hung up in it. What had I just gotten out of myself? Something spectacular maybe, something that I might have kept this time (I know I am lying to myself, but let me). Then it's gone. One flush. Not two.

Cecil's mom is in the bathroom now, damn her.

"You okay, honey?"

"Yes!" I yell. I am suddenly so pissed at her I shake. I bet it's the loss of blood. Then I think: I am not giving her the satisfaction. No way.

"I just had to pee real bad—you know how that is," I say. I'm bawling all of sudden, but real quiet.

Cecil's mom stands there silently and I think, "She knows but she don't want to tell me." I don't want to tell her either. I wonder if what happened made a secret smell, but all I can pick up is the smell of the commode.

"You sure?"

"Yes!"

Cecil's mom leaves the room.

A few minutes later I'm out of the bathroom, weak and dull-headed. But I still buy them DVDs. By this time Keanu and Liam have turned over a display of baseball cards and have purchased themselves horrible popguns. In other words, some old boy who runs the show has asked us to leave.

My mouth doesn't feel like it can work, like the blood it took to get rid of Number Seven came directly from my lips. We pull up to the Sugar Creek Nursing Facility, a bunch of brown brick buildings lying next to the bottom of the mountains, real close to the landfill place. Cecil's mom says to the boys, "Leave your guns in the minivan," and Keanu goes, "Fuck you."

Cecil's mom gives me the fruitcake tin of peanut-butter cookies, and then there's another great big spanking while me and Liam wait. It's gray and windy but not that cold any more. After the beating and after the guns are put in the minivan, we all go in.

Me and Cecil's mom and Keanu and Liam walk down a linoleum hall-way, and Cecil's mom greets every nurse and nurse's aide like she knows them. She's showing off how much she cares for her own mother by being all buddy-buddy with the staff. I just smile. I keep seeing the bloody nothing in the commode. I'm against abortion, always have been, but there it was—a fetus—and I just flushed it. I want to sob again but I know that's just stupid showing off. I need to let myself know that nobody gives a good goddamn what comes out of me, except maybe people who want to adopt babies and change their names and their lives and get them away from people like me. Yes, I know what I am. I have known that from the time you are supposed to know who and what you are, so please don't give me any goddamn looks.

I got that understanding burned into me with cigarettes and broken bottles and a few pushes down the basement stairs (oh hell, more than a few). My mom and her many men were always on my ass, letting me know how useless I was. "Practically retarded," they would say. I quit school at fourteen (I'm twenty-six now) and didn't find a job until finally this lady who owned a Hardee's let me work there. She paid me out of the drawer so she wouldn't get in trouble with the Tennessee Department of Labor. I just floated around the world in a Hardee's uniform with somebody else's nametag on it. But then I got pregnant by the boy who cleaned the bathrooms (you guessed it: Cecil) and had to quit. My mom disowned me and kicked me out of the apartment we shared, and I moved in with Cecil and his mom. Back then his diabetic dad was alive, poor man. He had a stroke but still made me and Cecil go get him Reese's Cups and Dairy Queen Blizzards with Reese's Cups whipped into them. "Eese's Ups," that's how it came out. And "Izzard."

I was pregnant! First time to give myself over to that, to be swollen up and almost hopeful. Me and Cecil got married after my mom signed some papers, but I don't think I loved him even then. I needed the marriage as a cover for my true love: the secret inside of me that everybody knew, the beautiful secret people could buy clothes, food, diapers, and toys for.

Cecil's granny is not conscious today.

Her chatty roommate and Cecil's mom are talking about how the city never buys enough salt for the roads in the winter. Liam and Keanu stand by the door. I'm standing by Cecil's granny's bed and she's breathing really hard like she can't find the right amount of air in her sleep. She's got yellowy silver hair pasted to her skull. Her body is thin as mop strings.

Liam comes over and takes my hand, but I don't want that right then, so I back away. He is a runt. He always gets ear aches. Keanu picks on him and I bet other kids pick on him too, and I just think I don't need his needy little hand right now.

Liam goes back to Keanu and then Keanu says kind of loud, "Quit crying."

Cecil's mom, who likes to baby Liam and beat up Keanu, goes over and picks up Liam and says, "Your great-granny is on her deathbed but she's going to Heaven, honey. No need to cry for your great-granny."

Cecil's granny's fat roommate goes, "Oh yes-sir-ree, honey. Your great-granny is almost there, sweetheart. Hallelujah. Hallelujah!"

She says "Hallelujah" about two thousand more times.

Then the old lady laughs a real loud funhouse laugh, and for a second or so I want to put a pillow over Cecil's granny's head because I wonder if she can hear how fucking stupid this all is. Maybe she'll see Number Seven up in Heaven, not a bloody nothing, but a fully-shaped boy or girl, pale and

Happy That They Hate Us

clean, in good clothes, with a backpack full of school supplies. Maybe Cecil's granny will walk this child to school on a crisp October morning.

Keanu says, "Look at the little crybaby faggot."

Cecil's mom, who's about ready to bust Keanu's butt again, goes "You shut your mouth, young man."

2

Cecil wants to burn down the trailer tonight.

This idea of his started when Cecil was driving trucks and fell asleep and ran into an embankment. He didn't get hurt but he totaled the semi. Now he's got a job at Bonanza Steakhouse pulling weeds and washing windows and just doing general steakhouse maintenance. He made a lot more driving trucks.

"Get the clothes you want to save. I'll help you pack your DVDs," he says, smelling like old water and cigarette smoke, still in his Bonanza maintenance outfit: a brown pair of slacks, brown shoes and a brown jersey. He's a big man with a gut and a half and long hair he thinks makes him look like Ted Nugent. But it's just a tangle of weeds in Ted Nugent's backyard that somebody needs to mow. Oh yeah, and add to your mental picture that he's crossed-eyed behind the thick glasses he has to wear. When I first laid my own eyes on him at the Hardee's, I knew me and him would have a relationship. He was looking at me with them crossed eyes like I was something he had never seen before, and yet I was nothing really. It's that sense of playing a trick that keeps me with him and also keeps me cheating on him at the same time, all the time.

"Not tonight," I go. "No burning down nothing tonight." I feel like mentioning my miscarriage, but hell he doesn't even know I got pregnant.

I'm putting the flea-market DVDs into my collection. For Christmas this year, Cecil got me a really nice shelf unit from Wal-Mart that can fit all my DVDs with space left over. I put *Vampire in Brooklyn* in between *Under the Volcano* and *Victor/Victoria*. I turn around and Cecil's standing there, looking at me like he does.

"I got it all worked out."

He's always talking about burning the trailer down and getting the insurance money. He thinks he has the perfect way to do arson, which is to turn over an electric heater by the washer and blame the fire on a short from the water flooding out the washer. Really I don't think they'd send fire investigators out for a $5,000 trailer anyway. I just don't need the inconvenience of setting the fire, moving stuff to a different location, lying and all that.

The funny thing is I want to go back to the BP right now and look around for the old boy who got me pregnant. It's this urge, like thunder inside my stomach and my head, this urge to repeat and repeat and repeat. But I'm too sore, and my body doesn't feel right.

"I'll help you pack up all your movies," he says in a singsong voice.

Somebody's knocking on the door. It's Phyllis, a neighbor. She wants to borrow *Pretty Woman* again.

"I should just buy it," she says. She's morbidly obese. She's always telling people that she didn't know she was morbidly obese till this year when the doctor told her for the first time. We'll be over at her trailer sometimes for supper and she'll lift a big spoonful of whatever to her mouth, saying, "Look at the morbidly obese woman eat her way to an early grave." Then she laughs, like as long as she has a sense of humor about it, being morbidly obese don't matter.

"Come on in, Phyllis," I say.

You can feel her weight stressing out the left side of the trailer as she climbs in. She's got on her maroon housecoat and sneakers, and her orange hair's cut real short. She just got divorced from a real skinny ex-con named Leonard who used to threaten to kill her. Phyllis would say that she ate so much because her layers of fat were like protection from him. "Emotional protection. I eat emotionally," she says sometimes. It's off *Oprah*, I bet. Sounds like it.

"I'm bored and I just love *Pretty Woman*. It lifts your spirits every time."

I pull out *Pretty Woman* and mark Phyllis's name next to where the title is written in my book.

"You are so damn organized, girl," she says.

Cecil laughs. "She can't balance a damn checkbook, but she sure can run her little free Blockbuster."

Phyllis scolds Cecil: "She is a treasure."

She comes over and hugs me like she's protecting me from him. But really it should be the other way around because, right then, I hate the both of them so much I want to flush them down the commode like Number Seven. It's just disappointment. It's just the way of the world.

"You know who is talking about you two again?" Phyllis says, looking sorrowful and yet pleased that she can deliver shitty mean-spirited news.

"Who?" Cecil goes.

Phyllis rolls her eyes way back into her head, holding onto the *Pretty Woman* DVD.

"Leland and Esther." Phyllis says the names like she is spitting up bad food, which is probably something she wouldn't do. I bet if you are an emotional eater you swallow anything that you can get your mouth around.

Leland and Esther live in the first trailer upfront and run the whole court. They take care of the mailboxes, putting Uncle Sam and American flag stickers on them for decoration, and they make sure the lots get sold if people leave. Leland used to be a preacher and Esther still plays piano in some church in Black Bottom. They are both holier than thou.

One time Leland came over to witness to me and Cecil. He said, "We all know, Gina, that you have had all them kids and have give them away and it's, well, in the eyes of God you are one of the biggest sinners in East Tennessee. You are shameless. You're going to hell."

Just all singsongy sweet, he said that shit, in his Home Depot vest, coming into our trailer and happily condemning me to hell. But guess what? A part of me appreciated his honesty. He laid it on the line, he said, because he could not live with himself. He needed to let me know how much of a monster I was so I could change into a wonderful human being. The "monster" part pissed Cecil off.

He said, "Leland, you can get the fuck out of my trailer right now, motherfucker. Who the fuck you think you are?"

"Someone who cares," said Leland.

"Get the fuck out, motherfucker!"

Leland just walked out. But since then him and Esther, who is short and round and going bald, have talked to people about us, about me, and I think it would make them happy to know what happened today. But I ain't telling nobody.

Phyllis says, "They are just hateful." She whispers it, wanting to stir us up and get something going at 8:30 on a winter Thursday night.

Which Cecil is about ready to do, but I get there first.

"I'm happy that they hate us!" I scream.

Phyllis looks at me like I just lost my cotton-picking mind.

"I am so fucking happy that Leland and Esther hate me and Cecil. We deserve their hate, don't we? We're the scum of the earth, aren't we? We are going to hell!"

I'm crying acid mean tears, but there is a true happiness in this outburst. A happiness that has never been in this trailer before, or maybe even in this world.

I stand there, breathing real hard, and Phyllis says, "Oh my goodness. Did I upset you?"

Cecil goes, "Honey, you okay?"

But I am not going to talk. I'm going to stare. I am going to feel anger burn its way out into reality the way a movie shines out of a TV screen. There's about thirty seconds of silence, and then Phyllis backs toward the door.

"Thanks for the movie," she says, almost in a whisper.

+

From down the road, just for a second or two, we watch the fire start to sneak out from the windows of the trailer. I've got every movie I ever bought in the trunk, in boxes and plastic garbage bags and paper sacks. That's all I took because, I told Cecil, I told him, I am sick of everything else I own. He said with the money from the insurance he would buy me new clothes at the mall and I told him, "Great, I don't care anyway." He took his KISS records and his KISS action figures and some of his jeans and his TV. That's all he cared about.

It went up quick: little box of nothing one minute, box of fire the next. As we watched, we let it get into our heads that we were okay people.

Cecil said, "Good riddance to bad rubbish."

He laughed and I did too. We got the trailer last year with money from his mom and our tax check.

"Let's go to Momma's and watch movies, you want to?"

+

Once we get to Cecil's mom's house, she says Phyllis, who is Cecil's mom's friend from high school, called to let her know the trailer was burnt down and that the police and the fire-people are looking for me and Cecil.

Cecil's mom says, "This is the last time I'm going to lie for you."

"Just tell them we was over here watching movies," Cecil goes. "They ain't going to be able to tell it was arson."

Cecil's mom laughs. "Oh you're so smart. It's the last time."

Keanu and Liam are already in their sleeper couch in the living room with the TV on the Fox News Channel. Keanu thinks the burnt trailer will be on the news, and I just laugh.

Happy That They Hate Us

"Honey, that's *national* news," I say, and he gives me the finger. I laugh some more because I am just so damn tired of everything.

Cecil's mom's house is way in the backwoods at the bottom of a mountain, next door to a couple who raise pit bulls. It's dark out, and you can hear a few dogs barking, but not as bad as usual. Cecil grew up in this house. His mom has kept his room, which is in the basement, just the way it was when he was little because, she said, she knew he was always going to end up coming back again and again. It's true. Me and him are always getting evicted or getting into big fusses and one of us or both of us wind up here.

"I'm gonna get five thousand from the insurance," he tells his mom.

He looks over at Keanu and Liam and goes, "Hey, boys."

They don't say nothing.

Cecil's mom is in a sweatshirt, sweat socks and the new pair of sweatpants she got at the flea market. She is sitting at the kitchen table looking through a shoebox of bills or pictures or something.

"I bet they'll send the cops out here," she goes.

Cecil laughs. "That's fine. I got a clear consciousness."

His mom looks up at him and frowns. "Don't be an idiot, Cecil."

Then she shakes her head.

Cecil goes into the kitchen with her to plead his case. He tells her that he has everything worked out, that the trailer had bedbugs and that there is no way in hell to get rid of bedbugs. That the trailer had formaldehyde in it like the ones the government supplied for the Katrina victims. That the trailer was not even worth *two* dollars, and he is going to get five thousand. That him and me will find a nice apartment in Johnson City and he'll get a better job and I can work too. It is the same story he always tells when we don't have a place to live, and for a second I hate him like everybody else does.

The boys are now watching some cartoon.

"I got all my movies out in Cecil's car," I say to them.

Keanu says, "You got *Transformers*?"

"Yeah, I got *Transformers*."

I swear to God that's all they want to watch.

Keanu gets out of the bed. He is in his underwear, so he puts on his pants and shoes and goes out to the car after getting Cecil's keys. Liam is smiling at me.

"What?" I say.

He just looks at me like he is happy to see me.

For some reason, I am so tired I cannot maintain my distance from him. I invite myself into the bed with him like I ain't the mom who gave him up to his granny. Like I am just his regular old mom, getting into the couch-that-makes-a-bed with him. He is under the covers, and I lie down next to him, and he scoots over.

"What?" I say, looking at him. He is still smiling. His face is small, and his eyes are great big. I've never really looked at him this close, except for the day he was born seven years ago. He is Cecil's. I know he is. He came out with a hard push from the other side of being alive, I remember, and I was split in two and then I came back together again. It is the circle of life, like in *The Lion King*. I got that one too.

I never have loved Liam, I don't think. I don't think I know how to do that. But right then, with Cecil going on about five thousand dollars and Keanu out getting the movie, I think how me and Liam could be the same age if we wanted to. We could walk together to catch the school bus and dress in matching outfits like twins. Getting on the bus and going to school can be a wonderful thing if you let it.

Liam says real quiet in his mouse-like way, "I'm glad you brought your movies. We don't have nothing to watch."

He reaches out to touch my hand but I pull back, just to let him know the only reason I am here is because there is no other place to go.

Happy That They Hate Us

Lowest of the Low

Barney's gone. I just heard his car door slam. I stick a frozen pizza in the microwave, go out on the patio, and look at the March sky, its cottage-cheese clouds, and those bony trees around the half-frozen field. Beyond that: the backs of a McDonald's and a Walgreens and the United Dairy Farmers where I work.

Barney's Tercel is out at the stoplight by the bank.

It doesn't matter. He told me upfront he wasn't really into me, and I kind of liked that. It took the pressure off. When I needed him, he was there, bored and glassy-eyed, embarrassed by how much I felt.

The other day he said his wife wanted him back.

"So you're not queer anymore?" I said.

"I guess not." He laughed. "She said she's pregnant."

I laughed too.

This is one of those deluxe frozen pizzas. Not bad. I eat half the thing and I smoke on the patio, with the TV on in my living room. I can hear the Wheel of Fortune and the overemotional audience. My apartment has some pretty nice amenities for being so crappy—a fireplace I don't use, brand new wall-to-wall carpet, a patio with sliding glass doors and vertical blinds. A washer-dryer combo in the bathroom. Too bad it doesn't work.

There's a knock on my door while I'm peeing. I yell that I'll be there in a sec. Of course, as I finish, I whip up a whole fantasy: Barney out there in the foyer next to the row of rusty robotic-looking mailboxes.

I open the door, and there's Tiffany, the teenage girl from upstairs.

"I'm sorry," she says. She wears a midriff Britney-looking thing and thick mascara, purple streaks in her hair. You can kind of tell that she's looking for something more out of life.

"Sorry for what?" I ask.

We don't talk that much. One time I helped her carry some groceries. Her and her mom's place was decorated with all kinds of funky shit, like a big cream-colored vinyl sectional sofa and ostrich feathers and an abstract painting with sparkling lights embedded in it, which they got on vacation in Gatlinburg.

"I have a favor to ask."

"Come on in."

But I am not in the mood. My boyfriend of three months just left me. I am a forty-two-year-old homosexual who day-manages a convenience-store. I have a major bald spot. I bite the crap out of my fingernails.

Tiffany and I sit down in the living room with *Entertainment Tonight* on.

"I need a lift over to my boyfriend's place. Mom's gone, and I don't have money for a cab, and it's just I really need to see him. He's been weird all day, calling me and begging me to come over, and I really think he's completely depressed, you know? I'm afraid of what he might do." She smiles like it's a joke, but it's not.

I do know "depressed." Hell, I know it intimately. I look right at her and I can feel tears starting in my eyes. I notice how she has a gut on her, poking out from the bright orange tee-shirt she's chopped in two to make herself look like a star. That little white belly breaks my heart.

"Let me get my keys."

She smiles, great big. I've seen her boyfriend before. Skinny as a rail with a wiry goatee and always in the same black tee-shirt and pants hanging down so you can see the Old Navy label on his underwear.

"You really are nice," she says.

I don't answer. I Saran-wrap my pizza, get my keys, and we're off. It's dark, and the little town is dead all around us, except for the drive-throughs. I look in at the convenience store I manage. There's Monique, the one woman I can't stand, running register, frowning like a mental patient, which she happens to be sometimes.

Monique once came up to me at the change of shift and said, "I saw that sticker on your car." Her expression was so serious as to be comical.

"What sticker?"

"That gay sticker." Monique frowned like a spy. She wasn't a Bible-thumper, just pissed and on the prowl for a target.

"Yeah," I said. It was a rainbow bumper-sticker Barney and me got when we went to Key West the month before.

"Aren't you afraid you'll get your brains bashed in? My cousin's gay, and he lives in Indianapolis and he got beat up last year. Him and his little boyfriend. I told him you can't be holding hands no matter what's on TV. *Will and Grace* or not, people can't take it."

The pitch in her voice was going higher. There's a certain kind of pleasure certain people take in letting other people know how dangerous it is for them to be alive. Monique had that going on big-time.

"I'd peel that thing off if I was you. I mean, come on."

Barney and me in fact met at the United Dairy Farmers. He was taking a second job to pay off credit-card bills. That first day he came on I trained him in. He came dressed in a pair of khakis and a short-sleeved shirt and a wrinkled clip-on necktie and scuffed-up Nikes.

"Am I late?" he said.

"No," I said, and right off I knew he was what I wanted. I saw his short dark hair, and the wrinkles in his tie, the wetness of his eyes and I knew.

I tried not to show it at first. I showed him how to change register tape and how to do inventories in back, where the mop sinks were. He followed along, real tired, you could tell, and after about two hours of training he said, "Can I smoke in here?"

I was pulling night-shifts back then. I had slept all day, so I was okay.

"No. But you can go outside and smoke if you need to. I'll watch the register. I'm a smoker too."

I grinned, and he nodded his head, went outside, lit up. I watched him from beside the Slurpee machine. He smoked like a little lost nobody, looking out at the parking lot as though he was staring at his own future and just seeing litter and oil-stains.

He came back in and said, "So where's the caffeine pills?"

"How about some extra strong black coffee?"

"Sure."

We drank French Roast and I showed him how to cut deli meats and how to arrange the donuts and how to check inventory and the bank deposit, all that. Then it was time to go home. He called his wife five times (they only had one car), but to no avail. She had fallen asleep.

"She sleeps like a corpse," he said, ringing out the mop. He looked down at the floor. There was a tiny piece of a candy wrapper floating in the mop water.

"I'll take you home."

Suddenly he was full of hope—like an insomniac just discovering some sleeping pills in a desk drawer.

At the stoplight just outside his apartment complex, Barney said he didn't want to go home.

"You wanna go get something to eat?" he asked. It was 5:00 AM.

"I guess."

"I really just don't want to see her," he said over scrambled eggs at the pancake house that used to be a Ponderosa, pig plaques and daisies on the wall.

I was drinking more coffee. I wouldn't sleep a wink I knew, and yet I felt him pulling me into his orbit just by being what he was: some sad-sack loser in a bad marriage having to work a second job to keep out of bankruptcy court. All his misery was giving him over to me.

"Where do you want to go?"

"I don't know," he said. Then he coughed, got his cigarettes out.

"So what's so bad about home?"

"Everything." He laughed and then his eyes were right on me.

"I have a couch," I said.

But of course that night he slept in my bed with me. I remember feeling like I had died and gone to some alternate universe. Not heaven, but close—a place where I got what I wanted without a lot of struggle. It wasn't a perfect world but it was somehow fair. Love got reciprocated right away. Love got love. He was what I wanted and he didn't pay a lot of attention to me while we did it, and when he got off it was like one single sad little pop and then he was unconscious beside me. I watched him breath for a long time. My eyes got hot while I watched.

Hell, I think I actually cried from happiness.

Barney moved in with me a few days later, and every day my life got easier because he was there, blank and willing to be the object of my desire. I didn't have to pretend that I could make it anymore. I realized what my main problem was, what had kept me in turmoil: just plain old run-of-the-mill loneliness. Of course, that realization would end up fucking me over in the end.

+

We're inside a condo over by I-275, on a cul-de-sac of beat-up-looking townhouses and condos, bags of garbage out front waiting to be picked up. The condo we're in is completely gutted, no furniture or nothing, boxes on boxes. Part of the living room wall has been karate-kicked in.

Beside the biggest hole, on the floor, is Tiffany's boyfriend, whose name is Kyle. It looks like he has not had a good day either. He's in sweatpants with no shirt and has the whitest skin, like he was born and raised in a basement in the light of video games. He has a tattoo of a demonic sun on his back, and he's wearing big black combat boots with no socks, strings untied. He just sits there, Indian-style, with his eyes focused on the paperclip he has untangled, trying to clean out his one-hitter so he can smoke more pot.

"His brother moved out last week," Tiffany whispers.

"Hey, you okay?" I say. When we came in, the door was half open and a cat was meowing beside the porch. The cat is in now, roaming the empty condo, smelling for its litter-box.

Kyle throws the used paperclip into the kicked-in hole in the wall. It's about the size of a mouth on a billboard. That must have taken a lot of karate kicks. His goatee beard has grown into a long strand spilling out of his chin. When he looks up, his eyes are a glittery fake gold.

"I'm fine. I mean, I'm getting fucking evicted tomorrow, but I am so goddamn fine." He laughs a messed-up-boy-on-a-soap-opera laugh then lights the one-hitter and inhales extra-deep.

Tiffany says, "Did you do that to the walls?"

"No," he says, and he laughs again that way, and he looks her right in the eye. "Jackie Chan did." His fake-gold eyes are contacts. They have to be.

Tiffany laughs too and goes over to him and sits down. He packs her a hit and she does it and looks up to me.

"He's gonna be homeless, Dwayne." She smiles with tears starting.

"I'm sorry."

Kyle stands and hands the one-hitter back to Tiffany. The only unpacked thing in the room is a boom-box on the floor, and he goes and turns it on. Hard rock from a whiny singer comes out. Kyle stands up again and feels his left nipple, then looks at me.

"Hey, you okay?" I say.

"I get pissed off all the time. I can't keep a job." He stares down at the floor.

Tiffany says, "When he goes low, you know, like from bipolar? I mean, when he goes low he is the lowest of the low." She stands up and sways a little. It looks like she's proud of Kyle's lowliness in a way.

I keep on smiling. I'm thinking of Barney. What he's doing. Are they ordering a welcome-home pizza from Papa John's? Are they talking about redecorating a room in their little house to turn into a nursery? Kyle steps closer and I can smell his bipolar body heat like an oven that's been on too long without anything in it. As he moves a wind blows past me and then he turns into the Karate Kid, connecting with a part of the wall that's not been demolished yet, his combat-booted foot going all the way through until half his body is in the adjacent kitchen and the rest of him is still with us. He lies there in the rubble.

Tiffany goes over to him, high as a kite now, but not laughing.

"Are you dead?" she says.

"No. Help me up."

He's breathing real hard. The bottom part of him is covered in drywall dust. His chest is bleeding little red stars.

"I hate my landlord," he says, like that might make me understand every-thing, and for a second I do. It happens right then of course, that feeling of love breaking in, a fist through a window. I look at Tiff for a second and feel sorry for her and sorry for me and just plain sorry for the whole damn world.

"You need a place to stay?" I ask.

He dusts off the legs of his sweatpants, stands up, smiles.

"Thank you, Dwayne," Tiffany says. She comes over and I smell that burnt-poinsettia odor of pot.

"Yeah," Kyle says. "Thank you, Dwayne."

Kyle and me and Tiffany share three weeks together.

Now and then, when she gets time, Tiffany's mom comes down to try and bring Tiff home. She's a skinny lady, with hardly any hair, in a pair of jeans and a Grateful Dead tee-shirt, glasses on a chain. She makes a lot of noise thumping down the stairs. She knocks on the door and yells Tiff's name. Me and Tiff and Kyle are usually in the dark living room watching rented DVDs. It's almost like we're a family, we're so quiet and disenchanted, Kyle laughing too hard at Jim Carrey. We eat whatever we want. Neapolitan ice cream and circus peanuts and beef jerky and Chinese food from a can. Each day at work I whip up decadent ideas in my head about what we'll be eating and watching that night. It's sick and yet it's also like hope.

One night, three weeks in, there's the thunder of Tiff's mom stomping down the stairs, and she pounds on the door. We're in the middle of *The Sixth Sense*, some very scary stuff.

"Tiffany," her mom yells. "You are coming home."

"Mom! We're watching a movie!"

She pounds more. This time she's had it. I am about to get up to face the music when Kyle pushes me back down, stands up, pauses the DVD, then half-stumbles to the door. He is in his underwear and nothing else. He opens the door.

"Why don't you fucking stop this shit?" He's yelling like he's on a reality TV show, like there's cameras everywhere and he has to put on some kind of act or get booted off.

I hear him yell and I can see parts of Tiff's mom out in the corridor. This time she's wearing cutoffs and her uniform top from Target. I'm feeling like I should disappear off the face of the earth. Her face is pale and tired and irate. She's not ready for a fight, doesn't even know if her daughter is worth saving. But then again that's all she's been doing lately, and it's become sort of second-nature.

"Get some clothes on right now," Tiff's mom says.

She tries to come into the apartment. Kyle won't let her though. Tiff looks halfway between wanting to protect her mother and wanting to go back to the movie. Turning to me and slumping her shoulders, she whispers, "This is weird. I love them both. It's like a tug of war for my heart."

Kyle keeps blocking the door like a goalie.

"Let me in. She's my daughter, goddammit," Tiff's mom grunts, growls almost. She goes from one side of the doorway to the other, but he's fast and he keeps her out. Finally she gets down on all fours and crawls through, knocking him back with her head. Once she's in, she runs toward us. It's dark except for the TV. I turn on the lamp. Tiff's mom is breathing real hard, standing beside the La-Z-Boy.

"I can't believe this," she says.

Kyle comes over and grabs her and slams her into the chair.

"I am so sick of you," he says.

"You're crazy!" she screams.

He hovers like he has trapped her with his secret powers and she will never be free. I slowly get up.

"Hey, you guys, come on," I say.

Kyle does not have his colored contacts in. His eyes are very brown, so brown as to be black. In his white Old Navy underwear he resembles a refugee from a nighttime tornado. He won't take his eyes off Tiff's mom. She's been targeted.

Tiff stands up now.

"We just wanted to finish the movie, Mom!" she screams.

Tiff is not in her underwear, but she might as well be—halter-top-thing, skin-tight jeans. I'm in my sweats. I must look sixty years old, all the bad food and hardly any sleep for the past three weeks, that feeling of being held captive by Kyle. He never leaves the house even though he keeps telling me that his brother is coming back to get him and that they are going to pick up Tiffany at school and escape to Arizona.

Tiff's mom is looking at me. "You ought to be ashamed."

Kyle comes to my defense: "He is a kind and gentle person." Kyle says that like it's so true it's downright embarrassing.

Hell, I've fallen in love with him and Tiff in a way, but I wish I hadn't. It's like they have come into my head and nested there, replacing normal life with their junk-food comfort and pot-head slumber. We drink beer and get drunk and they go into my bedroom and have their sex and I half-sleep out here and wake up and quietly get ready for work the next day, Tiff having slipped off upstairs, Kyle snoring like a cowboy with sleep apnea.

"Kind and gentle, my ass," Tiff's mom says.

Kyle's nostrils flare. "I will hit you, okay? I will fucking *hit* you, you pick on Dwayne!"

Tiff's mom looks away. "I just want my daughter."

Tiff runs over to her mom, bawling now.

"I'm sorry, Mom! He's bipolar."

Kyle starts crying too then. He goes over to the wall, makes a fist and punches a hole right next to the TV. This is the first time he's done that in here. The wall gives in like a piece of nothing.

"Time out," I say. I go over to Tiff and her mom, and I say, "Tiff, you go home with your mom. It's time to take a break."

Tiffany nods and gets up. Her mom stands, looking all hateful at me. "I ought to call Children's Services and the goddamn cops."

But I don't love them like that. My love is lazy and good-for-nothing, even possibly illegal, but it is not that.

"I'm not a pervert," I tell her.

She and Tiffany just walk out. Kyle is on the floor, not crying, just staring into space.

"Why don't you go to bed?" I ask him.

"I took my meds, swear to God," he says, still staring into space.

"I know you did. I'm the one that went and got them for you."

I walk over to the couch and lie down. Eventually he gets up and comes over to me.

"That stuff about my brother?" he says in the dark.

"Yes." I close my eyes.

"He never calls me. I made up that thing about Arizona. I'd like to go though. Maybe me and you and Tiff?"

Even with my eyes closed I can feel his smile. It's got the sticky warmth from not being able to live right. He wants me to take that smile in like a pervert would, use it to make myself happier than I ever should be.

When he bends down and kisses me, I just let my lips fold into my mouth, and then I open my eyes.

"Go on to bed," I say.

He stands there for a second or two, swaying.

"Whatever you say," he whispers.

+

Monique comes in at the end of my shift the next day. She gives me the evil eye.

"You don't look so good," she says. She's got the biggest ass in the tri-state area, wearing baggy sweatpants and a big smock to cover it.

It's close to 3:30 PM. While I am at work I try to do my job very well, thank you. But my clothes are not clean. I haven't gone to the laundromat in the past three weeks. I've been rinsing out stuff in the kitchen sink and then hanging it on the balcony to dry.

My shift is almost over. There's a smell of dirty bleach coming up from the floor I just sloppily mopped, from the fake-butter in the popcorn machine, from the waxy vapor of candy bars washed in sunlight.

"I feel okay," I lie.

"Are you sick?" she says, smiling.

"No."

"Well, you look sick." She stops smiling and goes over to the mop bucket I left in front of the milk coolers.

"Is this the water you used to mop with?" she asks, pissy and judgmental.

"Yeah."

"It looks like sewage." She laughs really loud.

Fuck you, I want to say. *Fuck this whole fucking world.*

+

After work I stop by Barney's place, which is cute and painted yellow and in a so-so neighborhood. He is out getting his mail. I sit in my car watching, half-camouflaged by the other cars and the sun light splashing through tree-limbs. I get out. He's opening some letter and smiling. He looks up.

"Hey," I say.

His eyes go cold. I must be smiling. Yes, I took a few "magnums." That's what Kyle calls his speed pills. I took a few around 1:00 o'clock because I was about to go into a coma. This is what love can do to you, I think right now, walking up to Barney, walking very slowly. My mouth hurts from how much I love him—maybe not hurt as much as burn. Yet I know how he can just leave without one thought about me and pick up where he left off.

"What are you doing here?" he goes.

"I don't know."

"Come on, Dwayne. Don't go Glenn Close on my ass." He laughs, but he's nervous, you can tell. "You look a little tired," he says.

"I'm very tired," I say, and I laugh too. But then I get choked up and stop.

"Come on," Barney says. "Leave us alone."

I stand there on the sidewalk. When he turns to go into the house I still don't move. He stops and looks back at me, gets a little pissed.

"Go home," he says. "Go on."

"I can't," I say.

This is embarrassing, I know, me standing there in the sunshine on the sidewalk outside his yellow cottage, him in some uniform, maybe UPS, I don't know. I can't move. There's a kind of hypnosis that comes over you when you're so miserable you can barely stand it. It pushes you into the center of a freeze-ray. Stubbornness sets in. You can do anything if you come to the understanding that you'll never get your way.

"It's over. Okay?" he is whispering, and he pulls my arm toward my car but I won't move. There is just no goddamn way.

I shake him off. I walk backwards.

"Go on," he says. "Get the hell out of here before someone sees you, freak."

Barney kind of laughs then, not a real laugh, but a cover-up. He looks both hurt and pissed, like he just can't understand my behavior.

"Have some fucking self respect," he says. Then he looks down the street both ways.

+

When I get home the door is wide open. Inside, furniture has been turned over. The walls are busted out all over the place. They look like Swiss cheese.

I get panicky and call out Kyle's name. There's no response. For a second, I think I might pass out. Then I hear a familiar stomping down the stairs. When I turn around, Tiff's mom is standing in the doorway. She looks like she wishes she had a gun.

"He did it," she says.

I can't talk right then.

"He beat the living shit out of my daughter," she says. "I just took her to the hospital, buddy. Thank God I came home for lunch. She was beat to a pulp over some stupid movie they watched. She's in intensive care. I come back to get her some things."

I still can't talk. She shakes the bag of her daughter's things in my face.

"He's gone. That little fucker took off. I called the police. They know about you too, buddy. What you were doing in there. It makes me sick. I don't have anything against gays, but I can't take a child molester. I cannot. I shouldn't have let this go on."

She keeps shaking the bag. It's clear plastic and inside it are a peach nightgown and some shampoo and socks and panties.

"I love Tiffany," I say.

"I am going to puke," she says and then glares. She looks like she would be the one at the front of the mob, the one who would start taking me apart limb by limb.

+

When Kyle comes back, he's all apologetic. It's around 8:30, and the police haven't come yet. He has on his combat boots and sweatpants and a suede jacket with fringes he told me his brother got him. He stands in front of me in the kitchen.

"Write me a check," he says.

"I don't think so."

"Please," he says, chewing gum real hard.

"No."

"Please, God, just write me a check!"

I shake my head and look him in the face He has a fierce, pathetic expression, something he practices I bet when he is all alone, pretending to be a lonely super-villain contemplating how bad off and evil he is. *Why doesn't anybody love me?*

"Let's go do laundry," I say.

His contacts are in. They glitter like gold fish. He looks like he doesn't understand.

"I don't have anything to wear to work tomorrow," I say.

"Everything I got smells," he says. He spits his gum out onto the floor.

We go around the apartment, picking up dirty clothes, and fill like seven big black garbage bags. I don't want to notice anything, the overturned furniture, the botched walls. Somehow Kyle is obedient, caught up in the need for clean clothes, like the boy he's supposed to be, vain and self-conscious. He carries four bags out to my car, and I carry the rest. I lock my door, and then we head for the Kroger's for some Tide and Bounce. We turn the radio on to his station. It starts to storm, and the rain is almost pretty on the windshield, like melting jewels.

The laundromat is just down the street, in a strip-mall next to a bar and a RadioShack. There's only one other person there, and she's reading a Harry Potter book in front of the dryers. There's a smell of mildew and clean clothes being dried. The plastic chairs are orange and green.

I give Kyle a five-dollar bill, which he slides into the change machine, staring like he's in a casino. There's happiness on his face, and his eyes are shielded with gold-drops. Maybe it's the lighting, but he doesn't look so ghoulish now. Like he has snapped out of something.

This needed to be done.

I sort and separate. Kyle puts in quarters, pours detergent. We sit down after everything is loaded—five machines in all. The woman with her book gets up and goes outside to smoke. The rain has stopped. The concrete and cars are glittery with what it left behind.

I turn toward Kyle, exhausted and for a second, almost happy with our accomplishment, all the machines going, the smell of detergent and hot water.

"Why did you hit her, honey?"

He doesn't say anything.

"Why?"

He sits there for a second, expressionless, like an android being asked a human question.

"Why would you hurt someone you love so much?" It sounds stupid once I say it.

"I didn't hurt nobody, Dwayne." His eyes are gold coins.

He gets up and smiles at me real big then.

"Can I get a pop?" he says.

I stand and give him a dollar. He walks over to the machines and chooses Mountain Dew. The clock says 9:15 PM. It's a Tuesday or a Wednesday. Hell, I don't know.

I Don't Know and I Don't Care

The day I got evicted, I simply loaded up my clothes in my gorgeous 1987 Ford Escort and ended up at the mall off I-70, the nice one. I had a twenty-dollar bill, so I went to the Starbucks, got myself a Venti Caramel Macchiato and sat my lily-white ass down. I sipped it and almost cried: the taste you want in your mouth the afternoon of your eviction. The mall made me feel pleasantly drowsy. I smelled the coffee and the air-conditioning and the perfume from an upscale store just a few yards off.

When the Starbucks lady left her post for a minute, all of a sudden I was the only person in the world, which not only gave me great comfort but also scared the shit out of me. So I wound up calling Crystal on her cell. I used the pay phone over by the bathrooms because I'd given up my cell last month and still owed a shitload to Cellular One.

A pale-faced teenage boy was hanging out by the men's room adjacent to the pay phones, in a pair of camouflage shorts and a red tee-shirt and flip-flops.

Crystal was about ready to quit her job at Subway.

"Well, I just got kicked out of my apartment."

I eyed the poor kid. He had short dark hair and little brown eyes, and I knew I had something to do.

"So you want to stay with me, right? Goddamn you, Kenny."

But she laughed. And I went: "We'll have a party, just me and you. I have sixteen bucks. You want beer or wine or what?'

"You don't seem worried. Um. Beer. Oh God, I am so sick of this place. I hate making sandwiches. People treat you like a goddamn slave!"

"Calm down," I said.

"I'm outside smoking. Nobody can hear me. Shut up."

She was laughing. The kid eyed me back. He went into the bathroom.

"Beer it is," I said. "What time are you off?"

"Right now."

"I'll be there in half an hour."

"Hurry up. Fuck it. I'm quitting."

I went into the mauve and silver bathroom. He was in stall number two, the one for the handicapped, with the door half open. I guess you can take it from there.

+

Crystal and me met at a job we both quit. Taco Bell, I believe. Not a place you want to work. We hit if off from the start though, joking around all night long, getting high in the bathroom, making mixed drinks in to-go cups—cheap vodka and Dr. Pepper, cheap rum and Mountain Dew. She has a big mouth and is taller than me, bigger-boned, but her face is little-girl and her voice has that high-pitched girly sound big ugly guys in bars like. We're both twenty-four, have done nothing with our lives, and we'll say that shit to people right out loud. We both like hard rock. But the one time we had tickets to Metallica we got too fucked up on the way and ended up laughing next to a cornfield.

That, of course, was the night I told her I was a fag. She laughed hysterically. I was all serious. Sometimes I actually think people can't tell, like I could pass as a non-fag. Even though I am a little, shall we say, sissified, I don't wear flashy clothes or work out all the time, God knows, or listen to techno music or even watch the queer shows on TV.

"What?" I said that night. We were on some back-assed road, smoking the pot we'd bought for the show, both in black tees and black jeans and black boots.

She stopped laughing.

"I knew the minute I saw you, hon."

I must have looked hurt because she got real close to me in the car. Her breath had that home-cooked smell of pot.

"It made me fall in love with you even more," she said. She was serious too. I suddenly felt obligated and surrounded, but that only made our connection sloppier, like we were swimming in a polluted pool.

"Shut the fuck up," I said.

She slapped my face but not that hard.

"I've got ludes," she said.

"Can I have a drink of your pop?"

We did finally make it to Metallica, by the way. An hour late, but we made it.

+

The kid's name was Jason. He gave me his phone number on a paper towel. He had a Sharpie, which he probably brought to use on the stall walls. He said he was home all the time and had been bored all summer. You could tell he was lonely, and not just because he had the weak white complexion of a science experiment gone a bit awry.

"Thanks," is what I said.

Then someone came in and we scattered. He disappeared down the corridor toward the Cinnabon. For a brief minute or two, I got that rush of love you only get when people walk away from you real fast.

+

Crystal's fat ass was out on the sidewalk smoking. She was in her brown Subway smock, a white tee-shirt and jeans, her brown hair pulled out of its rubber band. When she saw me, she gave me the finger.

"What took so long?" she said, getting in, slamming the door. Her car was dead somewhere.

"I had to finish my Caramel Macchiato."

"You motherfucker," she said, slapping me. "Did you even think about getting me one?"

"I'm buying you beer, so shut up."

She laughed.

"Thank God. You know what else? I got my last paycheck from Fuckway." She pulled it out. "Two hundred and twenty-seven dollars. That's for two weeks of slave labor."

Crystal kissed it and put it back. I stopped off at the beer place we always go to and got what we needed. On the way to her house, a one-bedroom shack that she rents from her mom's ex-boyfriend, she asked me about my boyfriend leaving and me getting evicted and how I was feeling.

"Like crap."

But to be honest, Robbie was just a drug dealer who I knew and sucked off. Groceries were my responsibility and rent was his, but I didn't usually get the groceries and he obviously did not pay the rent. At the beginning, though, during the going-to-Goodwill-and-buying-furniture part, we were kind of close.

"Poor thing," Crystal said. "Man, I'm telling you, Kenny—we need a vacation."

"Where?"

"I don't know. Gatlin…"

She was about to say "Gatlinburg," when I turned the corner toward her house, which sat between two others, one abandoned, the other up for sale. She did not finish her sentence. Her eyes got real big. I looked out. In fluorescent orange spray-paint someone had written all over the front of Crystal's place: *Cocksucking nigger lover!!!*

I shit you not.

When I pulled into her gravel driveway and asked her who did this, she said: "I don't know and I don't care!"

She was laughing at first. Then she was crying.

"I haven't seen Darrell in two weeks!" she said through the sobs. He was the black cook she'd dated when she was working at Applebee's. They were hot and heavy for a while, till Darrell took off with his used-to-be girlfriend.

"This is so shitty," I said.

The letters were smeared and drippy, their color beating at my eyes off of the beige siding. Even the glass of the front window was painted over. The exclamation marks were sweetie-pie curlicues, almost like seahorses.

We just sat there. Are you supposed to get out and start scrubbing when something like this happens? Get out of your car and raise your fists to God? What? I'd never been a victim of this kind of thing. I mean, my car was stolen once, and someone beat the crap out of me at a party because of a smart remark, but this was way, way over the top. I felt like we should want revenge. But the sight of the defacement, decorating Crystal's house with somebody's pure spite, was just too much sadness to take on a hot, humid Tuesday, with the sky blank but bright.

"I'm not going in there," Crystal said. She had stopped crying, but her face was pathetic. She looked like the little girl her squeaky voice always betrayed her to be.

"Should we call the police?" I asked.

She looked away from her house.

"I have had it!" she screamed. "I don't want no police! I don't care! Get me the fuck out of here now!"

I backed up the car and we rode around out near the strip mall that had hardly anything but a Save-A-Lot, a discount shoe store and a check-cashing place.

"Pull in," she said.

I did.

"Park."

After she wiped her face on her hand and her hand on her jeans, she got out. It was hot. I rolled down my window and turned on the radio. She went into the check place and came out later with some cash.

While putting her seat belt back on, she said, "Darrell was sweet to me."

"We've got beer."

"He was cute, too," she said.

"Yes, I know."

She started crying again.

"I should be pissed, but I'm just plain sad," she said.

"Yeah."

I backed the car out and turned up the radio. Some song by Korn. She got us beers. I was close to the interstate, thinking we might use some of her Sub-way money to eat out, but then she told me to turn as we passed a Holiday Inn Express parking lot. Almost brand new. In-ground swimming pool in front, Outback Steakhouse to the left and a Max and Erma's to the right. The sign out front said: *Free internet access and continental breakfast buffet.*

We parked and then walked into the lobby. A flabby guy behind the mahogany front desk asked for a credit card, which Crystal didn't have.

"I do have cash," said Crystal. "Here, take my driver's license."

She smiled with all her teeth, which totally made the guy suspicious. Then he looked at me. Thank God we'd parked off to the side so he couldn't see my crappy car. But he was young and tired. When Crystal paid him for one night with her Fuckway money, he just took it, gave her two card-keys, said have a nice stay and went back to his computer. He was doing something on eBay.

The first thing I noticed in our room (214) was the A-C smell coming to life in my nasal passages. I felt like I was in some weird and beautiful dream. There were dark green bedspreads and crisp off-white window treatments and a big desk and night stands and a TV with a remote and a phone with a little red light on it. The smell, though: pure and clean, like you could wash yourself in the air and come out brand spanking new, not even remembering who the fuck you once were.

Crystal flopped down on the bed, grinning.

"Now this is what I wanted," she said. "Some place to get my shit together."

She stared up at the ceiling, and I flopped down on the other bed. The pillows were huge.

"Go get the beer," she said.

By the time I got back, she was talking to Darrell, crying and putting on a cell-phone drama.

"I don't know, Darrell!" She had taken off her uniform and was in her bra and panties on the edge of the bed. The TV played silently. Oprah was interviewing Sarah Jessica Parker, the chick from *Sex and the City*.

"I said I don't know. But it hurts, baby. Have you ever had your property messed with? Huh? I know... Shit! Racism! This is so fucking horrible! I know... I know... Yeah."

She went on, turning away from me toward the wall, whispering. She was going to use the whole incident to rekindle romance. I popped a beer can open and sat down and turned the sound up a little. Sarah Jessica Parker was talking about her husband, Matthew Broderick, and how even though you might consider her to be a liberated lady she liked to make him a big breakfast some mornings. I listened to Crystal giggling and felt kind of sick.

So I went out to the pool, which was empty. The blank dead-white sunlight smacked into everything: tables, white umbrellas, black concrete. The chlorine smell mixed in with the heat. I wanted to know what to do next. The feeling inside me was as empty and yet filled up as the pool.

As I went back toward the room, I shoved my hand into my pocket in search of a little wadded-up paper-towel. Jason's number. The kid in the bathroom. At the pay phone in the front lobby I put in two quarters, while being watched by the guy behind the desk.

Some lady answered.

"Is Jason there?"

She yelled for him, and Jason came on a few seconds later.

"Hey. It's Ken. You know, from the mall today?"

"Hold on."

He said something to the woman and then picked up another extension. I heard the other phone clicking off.

"Wow. You called." Whispered voice.

"Yup."

"Why?"

"I don't know."

"I'm glad you did."

"Thanks."

"Man, I am bored," he whispered, and then he laughed.

"Where are you?"

"West Chester."

The suburbs, just down the interstate. He gave me directions and I went without telling Crystal. We arranged to meet at the front of his housing addition so his mom wouldn't see. When I got there, he was standing in front of a big stone fence, behind which were massive granite and aluminum-sided mansions with SUVs and green grass. I pulled over and he jumped in. My car died. I started it again. We were off. He was quiet, smiling. We got back on the interstate and I looked over at him—a geek, to tell the truth. Gangly and pale with brown hair and acne. Old Navy tee-shirt and camouflage shorts and flip-flops. His eyes were on me.

"I can't believe you called me."

"I know." I laughed, and we got off the interstate, passing the Holiday Inn Express.

For some reason I drove to Crystal's house. All the way there we shot the shit with dumb little statements about how hot it was and how his mom was a part-time church secretary and his dad an insurance salesman, how he

I Don't Know and I Don't Care

was sixteen and liked *Lord of the Rings*. When I finally pulled up in front of Crystal's place, he saw the bright orange words glowing like radioactive puke and said: "My God."

I stopped the car.

"Some asshole did this to my best friend," I told him, and I actually got choked up.

We went up to the slab of concrete that was her porch, passing a bird bath with a car battery in it. Her mailbox had an American flag decal. But the words of course drowned out all of that detail.

"Where's your friend?"

"In a motel. She had a nervous breakdown when she saw it."

"I bet. I would too."

I smelled the hot stink of spray-paint. Inside the window I saw Crystal's couch, covered in dirty clothes.

"I bet we could paint over that," Jason said.

"With what?"

"Get some house paint, you know, that matches the siding. I bet we could."

"You got any money on you?" I asked.

He looked scared. "A little."

"Enough to buy some paint and brushes?"

He nodded.

"I mean, we'll pay you back. It's just, you know, I bet you're right. We could paint over it for her. I mean, she was devastated. You sure you don't mind?"

"No."

He smiled at me, like we each knew what kind of person the other was. We went to Home Depot, got some beige exterior paint and a roller and a brush and pan. Close to 6:00 PM we set up shop and went to work, painting over the words. We got into a weird hot trance and almost started competing. But in the end, we stood back and saw that everything just looked even more pathetic—like two dumb-ass faggots tried to paint over what the cocksucking nigger-lover deserved.

I smiled, panting.

"It looks like shit," I said.

Jason cracked up. We stood there in Crystal's yard laughing like idiots. A train roared by, big horn going off, but we still kept laughing.

+

We went to the Holiday Inn Express, after getting milkshakes at Dairy Queen. I used my card-key to get into Room 214, and when we walked in Crystal was still in her bra and panties. But this time Darrell was on the bed with her, in his white underwear. Big black dude with a gut, shaved head, goatee. The only light was coming from the TV. They were watching some reality show where people have to eat crazy shit to stay in the game.

Crystal sat up. Me and Jason came in.

"Where'd you go?" Crystal said and then went, "Who's that?"

"Jason."

Darrell laughed with a real deep-pitched voice, eyes ablaze in the glow off the TV.

"Is that Kenny?"

"Yeah," I said.

"Is that Kenny with one of his little boyfriends?" He laughed a belly laugh, and Crystal told him to shut up.

I could tell Jason was a little freaked. I closed the door behind him anyway. We stood next to the empty bed while someone on TV ate lamb guts.

Crystal got up and put on her Subway smock.

"Hi, Jason," she said and coughed.

Darrell said, "They staying the night?"

Crystal turned around. "If they fucking want to."

"Fine with me." Darrell sat down, belly hanging over on his legs. "I don't care if you're queers, but just wait till I go to sleep to do anything. Or maybe just do it in the bathroom, real quiet." He grinned, with meanness coming out. That's what Crystal always likes in a guy.

Crystal came over and looked me in the eye, turning on a lamp.

"I know," she whispered.

"What?" I said.

"I shouldn't have called him." She mouthed that.

Jason just stood there next to me. Darrell put his shorts back on.

"I can't believe people are so fucking stupid, doing that to her house," he said. "Fucking hillbilly racists, man."

"We went over and tried to paint over it," I said.

Crystal smiled "You guys did that?"

"Yeah."

I Don't Know and I Don't Care

Jason was completely quiet. I noticed how young he looked, and then Darrell lit up some crack, which had a gas-grill-mixed-with-burning-plastic smell. He gave Crystal a hit.

"You guys want any?" she asked after her eyes quit rolling.

"No," I said.

Darrell went into the bathroom and shut the door. He started singing a song real loud. Crystal lit up the crack pipe again. When Darrell came back out, he looked crazy but sweet. He got back on the bed and put his arms behind his head. But his legs shook bad. He had stretch-marks under his arms from gaining weight and losing weight and gaining it back.

Darrell shut his eyes and opened them. Looked right at me and Jason.

"Bathroom is now free, gentlemen."

We both went in as if we'd been ordered. Me and Jason stood in front of the huge mirror, which was surrounded in dull-yellow globes of light. The floor was mosaic tile, real pretty. I looked at Jason in the mirror.

"What did you tell your mom you were doing tonight?" I asked his reflection.

"Staying all night with this guy named Brian."

What if she calls Brian to check on you?"

"I guess I'll get into trouble." He smiled. Then he stopped.

We just stood there. I mean, earlier in the day we'd been going down on each other at the mall, but in the bathroom we were tired and covered in paint. When he leaned over and kissed me, I felt like I knew him better than I'd known anybody in my life, like we'd been Boy Scouts together. We kept kissing and then got naked and went in the shower and did what lovebirds like us do.

+

Once we dried off and got back into our clothes, we went out into the room. Crystal and Darrell were getting it on in a drugged-up stupor. We were so tired we just slipped into the bed. They were loud, but the TV kind of drowned them out. Jason crawled up against me, and we tried to go to sleep, even with the two Tasmanian Devils next to us.

Then a few minutes later Jason whispered, "I think I want to go home."

I looked at him in the blue TV light. The fucker was crying.

"What?"

Crystal and Darrell kept on.

"I want to go home."

I kissed him and he stopped crying and got out of bed and stood by the door with his hand on the knob. I thought Darrell said something, but I didn't want to know what it was.

Outside it was still muggy and the pool was empty. The lights off the interstate looked like pills being swallowed. Jason went to the car without a word. It was like he ate too much candy or rode one too many rides at an amusement park. I drove him back to his house and dropped him off at the stone fence, as he requested. He opened the car door and turned toward me, like he was about to apologize, but then he just smiled like you might smile at a death row inmate about to be led off to his/her demise.

"Bye," he said.

"Yeah."

He walked off into someone's backyard, and I started to back up. But then I stopped, put the car in drive and pulled into his housing addition. It was called Oak Hills. All the homes were lit with beautiful security lights, and all the windows shone. Paved driveways and huge mailboxes. I drove through real slow, and I saw Jason running toward his house. We made eye contact, and he looked pissed, like I was betraying him. I revved my engine like a badass. Of course it died.

I pumped the gas pedal a few times and got this terrible feeling like I was going to get caught by these fine upstanding citizens and piss my pants in front of them. I was not of their ilk. I pictured them coming out to execute me. Maybe I just wanted to kill all of them, even though the only one I knew was the kid who just sucked me off at the Holiday Inn Express. But I hated him just the way he hated me just now when I would not disappear. I pumped the gas pedal real hard, a loud couple of thumps, kept turning the key in the ignition. There's this anger that I only feel when I get beyond who I am and what I have done and what has been done to me, when I truly understand the world and all its bullshit, when I *know*.

Right when I was about to say fuck it and get out and go on some kind of suburban rampage, though, the old Escort started, and I just pulled out.

+

When I got back to the motel, Darrell was gone. Crystal was on the bed, half-asleep, with the TV going. I crawled in with her.

"Darrell had to go meet somebody or something," she said. "I don't think he'll come back tonight."

I Don't Know and I Don't Care

She touched my face real softly, like a mom on a TV show. I kissed her on the cheek like a true gentleman. I was suddenly very happy, surrounded by her and the clean sheets, that A-C humming. She relaxed into her pillow, closing her eyes, and then she started to snore.

+

Outside, around 2:00 in the morning, I climbed the little fence around the pool.

The hours were posted and it was closed. The lobby clerk might see, but I didn't care. I was in my underwear and I dove in, went all the way under. It was warm and I thought maybe this is where I belong, underwater, like a baby whale. Then I remembered the time when I was a little kid, maybe seven or eight, and my dad took off on a bender and the electricity got shut off in our apartment. Me and my mom and my big sister were just sitting in the dark when my mom said, "Come on, kiddos," laughing under her breath because she had just about fucking had it. She was a little crazy anyway. We went to this motel, this funky old Sheraton Inn. It was 1986 and we watched *Miami Vice* in our room and we had Burger King and we went to the pool. I remembered feeling like I was The Shit, this little no-good kid with his mom and sister in the water with him.

I wondered what had happened to them. Where the fuck had they gone? I wondered if you can make yourself into anything you want just by holding your breath, just by wishing yourself into another world. But right then, of course, I had to come up for air.

Don't Be a Stranger

I

After the threesome, we went to the Bonanza Steakhouse on Route 5. Elaine and I were not hungry, but Kurt was. Plus Kurt and I both wanted to see what the place looked like now that it was remodeled.

Kurt and Elaine and I went in and got our trays and silverware. The smell on the way up to the pop station was the same smell I remembered from five years back when Kurt and me worked the dish room together: bleach vapors mixed with the smoke of burning meat. I got this rush of nostalgia about us getting high in the bathroom and going out after work to the bowling alley in McCordsville or to the movies or even to that one gay bar in Dayton. I made a suicide at the pop station, taking a hit from each variety, and then I grabbed a straw and sucked down about half the glass.

Kurt, skinny and tall, had on a black skullcap and a black concert tee-shirt with a flannel over it. Elaine wore a short jean skirt and a purple blouse and her leather coat and high heels.

Kurt turned and yelled at me after he got his pop, "Remember that time I had to mop up the puke in the dining room? It was projectile, man. That shit hit the ceiling."

I laughed. He was always trying to be shocking and foul-mouthed in public, like he was videotaping his own secret version of a *Jackass* movie.

"What a world," Kurt said, and he smiled at me like he was happy we were all together.

Elaine pulled the thingy on the iced-tea machine. She was very quiet.

It was a Thursday in January, and hardly anybody was around. The place had reopened about four months back. The menu board had the same pictures from five years ago, of baked potatoes and a big old lovely T-bone and an imaginary heavenly salad bar. But the fluorescence from the bulbs had faded the photos blue. Behind the dessert case a fat teenaged boy in a chef's hat stood in front of the grill, which had a couple pieces of meat on it, while some midget-looking gal ran rolls out to the salad bar.

At the cash register was a skinny woman in a purple pantsuit, looking above it all even though she worked at a Bonanza.

"What'll you have?" she said.

"T-bone. Medium rare," Kurt said. It was the most expensive thing, and Elaine was going to be pissed. She was paying.

"You want sour cream on your baked potato, sweetie?" the lady asked.

"Hell, yes."

Elaine asked the lady if she could have the kid-sized chicken-fingers dinner because she wasn't really hungry, but the woman said sorry, no. So Elaine just got the adult version. I said I'd have the chopped steak.

Once we sat down at a table, Elaine started talking about how she and Kurt were going to have a Super Bowl party. She said it fake-happy, like she was trying to wake herself up with her own voice. Her hair was pulled back tight with a rubber band and you could see the dark roots.

"I'm buying a flat-screen TV or maybe rent one," she said.

Kurt was eating some crackers he got off the salad bar.

"What?" Kurt said.

"Rent a flat-screen TV."

"Just buy it," he said.

I go, "Yeah."

"Where's our fucking food?" Kurt barked.

"It's coming," said Elaine.

Kurt lit a cigarette. The skinny lady in the pant outfit came over and told him there was no smoking. She called him "sweetie" again. Kurt apologized but didn't put his cigarette out.

Elaine asked him to.

Another gal brought our food out.

Kurt kept smoking. He ate and smoked at the same time. He looked so damn happy.

I cut my steak and looked at Elaine. She was eating her chicken fingers real fast, like an animal that knows another animal is in the vicinity.

"This is good stuff," Kurt announced.

He understood he could get away with things, and he also understood that people like me and Elaine would always be there, the kind of people who liked the feeling of being used. It was one of the only ways we knew we were alive. Sometimes he was this fun-loving high-school dropout who wanted to please you with his bullshit and who talked about going on Jerry Springer to kick his stepdad's ass. But he also read Harry Potter books aloud to us at night with a fake English accent because he said we watched too much TV.

I'd been living with them, sort of. But that night I was going back to my apartment.

"I'll make that chili I make for the Super Bowl party. With the hot peppers in it. Burn your fucking mouth off," Kurt said, lighting up another cigarette. The cashier kept on staring at him.

Then he made total eye contact with me, and I could see myself through his eyes all of a sudden: skinny, tall nobody with black hair that was too long.

"Sir," the cashier lady said from behind her stand.

He just ignored her, still looking at me.

"That extra hot chili with chipotle peppers."

He took a bite of steak.

The teenaged cook came out and said, "Sir. You can't smoke in here. It's Ohio law."

Kurt exhaled smoke in a big strong line.

"Sorry," he said. But he still didn't put it out.

Elaine reached across the table and grabbed the cigarette right out of his mouth, put it out in her own glass of iced tea. Kurt sat there like a kid whose name had been called over a loudspeaker at school. Elaine wiped at her mouth with her napkin. The cook went back to his grill.

"Fuck you," Kurt said to Elaine. But he didn't move at all, like he was frozen. After about a minute he went, "I'm sorry."

Elaine got up and went to the bathroom.

"Do you want to go back and watch the footage?" Kurt said.

I just smiled.

"Do some more?" he said.

In my head I saw Elaine's sweaty face while he was doing it to her. I was naked and trying to make sure I had pressed the right button on the video camera, pretending I liked making threesome-porn. Elaine's expression was like a doll's under a bed, like she was hiding but had no idea she was hiding.

"No, I got to work tomorrow," I said.

"Okay."

Elaine came back. We left. They dropped me off at my place. As I got out of the car, Kurt turned around and said, "Don't be a stranger!"

He laughed real loud and then peeled out.

2

Rocky got out of the psych unit last night. Now he's sitting in his chair in the big long den of the house where four other retarded people live. Rocky is black and always pissed off. He only says a few words, yes or no, mainly. He's humming kind of loud right now, smelling the fingers on his left hand.

Jeremy, the group-home manager and my ex-boyfriend, is at the dining-room table off to the side, doing paperwork. Molly, the girl with Down syndrome who doesn't know where she is anymore, is at the other end of the table, looking down at the place where her plate of food used to be. She's always hungry and has the reddest hair. The other ones—Dick, Katharine, and Rose—must be in their rooms.

Jeremy looks up at me and smiles but you can tell he doesn't like looking at me. We were living together up till I ran into Kurt and Elaine a couple months back. It's kind of uncomfortable now. But he's professional and okay to me because I'm the only one who shows up for his shift regularly.

Jeremy goes, "I've got sheets and towels in the dryer, and they all had their 6:00-PM meds and dinner, so tonight should be a breeze. Rose's mom picked her up to take her to a play or something, but Dick and Kath are already in bed and here's Molly and you-know-who got out of the psych unit just as sweet and personable as ever."

Jeremy has on sweats like heavy people wear. He is bald and his head is shaved all the way now so he looks at little scary, like the uncle on *Addams Family*.

"Cool," I go, walking over to Molly.

She looks up with spit all over her mouth. "Swiss steak."

Jeremy goes, "We already had the Swiss steak Miss Molly."

But she keeps saying it, so I smile at her and get her a glass of diet pop. She drinks it down real fast, and then belches and says "Swiss steak" again.

Jeremy yawns and stretches.

"I'm on till 9:00 PM, but I don't think you'll need me."

I think back to yesterday when I was doing the threesome with Kurt and Elaine, and I wonder if Jeremy can tell what a pervert I am just by being around me. But then again, who is he to judge? He's a fag too and used to send me flowers and make huge old-fashioned southern dinners like his mom would make (he's originally from Kentucky). Fried chicken and mashed potatoes and one time he did it in an apron but he was naked underneath and acting like a big fat sexpot in his little apartment kitchen.

"Sure. Everything seems peaceful."

I walk into the den and Rocky is still smelling his fingers, humming, and there's a radio on in Dick's room. The TV is off because Rocky does not like it on. Ever. He got taken to the psych unit about four days ago because he pulled the TV out of the entertainment center and slammed it into a wall. You can still see the damage by the sliding glass doors. He just missed the glass. The TV was ruined and they called and had him sent to the unit. I wasn't here, thank God. I don't like to see Rocky that way. I kind of like him.

That radio is playing Martina McBride. Dick is probably dead to the world. It's only 7:00 PM, but he is such a morning person he'll be up at 4:30 tomorrow, ready for his instant oatmeal, dressed for workshop with his lunch in his backpack. He's tall and has a little part of his head missing from some kind of washing-machine accident when he was seven.

Katharine is probably in her room writing things in her notebooks. She comes home, and eats, and then gets ready for bed and spends most nights in her bedroom doing her "paperwork." She likes to call it that. She just writes her signature and a bunch of numbers over and over, even if there's no ink in her pen.

I turn on a floor lamp and sit down on the brown vinyl sofa. Then the dryer goes off down in the basement and, as I get up, I hear a little scream. It gets tangled up in Rocky's humming. I go over to the sliding glass and look out back. There's a security light over a torn-up basketball hoop and, up next to the house, is a bunch of crap that wouldn't fit into our shed: an old wheelchair and an upside-down chair from Dick's room that he used to pee on.

I hear the sound again. It's more like a baby laughing now. I open up the sliding glass door.

Jeremy gets up and comes out. When I bend down beside the brown chair Dick ruined, I see the four of them inside where the chair had been turned upside down, nestled on a cushion: a smoke-colored momma cat with two black kittens and one orange one.

"Crap," Jeremy says.

The kittens are eating from the momma cat's titties. They are so hungry it looks like it hurts the mom to feed them. But they don't stop. The momma cat hisses again, and the orange kitten stops eating. Its eyes are still closed, but it hisses too, like it's imitating her.

"We can't have cats here," Jeremy says.

I stand up, my palms mud-covered. The kittens have stopped eating and are mewling again.

Jeremy goes, "Rocky, don't come out here, hon."

The only light is from the big street lamp above the basketball hoop and the light that comes through the sliding glass doors, where Rocky is standing, hands on his hips, looking at what we're looking at. Then in his pajamas and sock feet he walks out on the muddy yard and points down at the chair, while the cats mewl and squirm. He lets out a big howl. Jeremy and me know not to do anything but let him ride it out. Then he turns real quiet, still pointing at the cats, his finger shaking.

Dick and Molly and Katherine are now looking out too, all in their pajamas. A car pulls up into the driveway. It's Rose and her mom in her Cadillac. Rose's mom is rich, has dyed blonde hair, and is about seventy years old. Rose is big and pale and full of love. She has a plastic bag from Target in her hand.

"What's going on?" Rose's mom asks.

Jeremy says, "We have a cat and three kittens now. They've made themselves a home out here, Mrs. Daniels."

Rose says, "Look, Mom."

I go over to Rocky to help him back inside, but once he sees me coming he runs back into the house. Dick and Catharine and Molly scatter so he can come in.

Mrs. Daniels says, "Jeremy, if you'd have all this stuff taken to the dump you wouldn't have a problem." She lights a long cigarette.

Rose goes, "Can we keep them?"

Jeremy laughs. "Oh no. I'll call the shelter and see when I can take them in."

I walk into the house then to make sure Rocky is okay.

Molly says, "Swiss steak?" This time in question form.

Dick and Catharine are at the sliding glass doors, staring out like there's a whole new world now with the cats and everything.

I knock on the bathroom door and Rocky doesn't say anything. So I try the knob and it's open. Rocky's in there with the light on, sitting on the floor, sobbing. He looks like an old man who just lost all his possessions in a big fire. I get down on the floor. Rocky stares at me as he cries, unable to tell me what's on his mind, but somehow I think I know. It's something to do with his shut-tight personality and the TVs he smashes and the psych unit and being stuck here with all of us and wanting something else but not knowing what that is. So he's always frustrated and ready to cry and then suddenly there's a new litter of kittens in his back yard, coming out of nowhere, given to him maybe by God, and he just can't take it.

"Oh, honey," I say. Sitting on the floor, but not touching him. He'd go off.

3

One night five years back, not long before the Bonanza closed down, I was in the dish room running the day's final set of dishes. Back then, Kurt and I were sharing an apartment close to the Bonanza so we could walk to work if my car fucked up which was most of the time.

But Kurt was no longer working at the restaurant. He'd quit a week before and had been investigating the possibility of being a small-businessman with his stepsister in Indiana. They were trying to pull together a meth lab out in the middle of nowhere in his stepsister's grandma's abandoned house. He'd gone over there to scope things out a few days prior, and was supposed to be back. Then the call came. It was Regina, his stepsister, and her voice was just pure terror.

"He's sick, Nathan," she said. "I'm at a pay phone at the Arby's. It's bad."

"Sick how?" I was holding onto the mop, the skinny lesbian manager with frosted hair looking real cross because she wanted to get the fuck home.

"I don't know. Coughing up blood."

"Damn."

"We were over at Granny's house and it's cold and he's hot as hell and don't want to move, but he keeps saying your name."

She laughed, like someone saying my name when they're real sick was a big joke.

"I'll be there in an hour," I said.

I had the 1982 Chevy Citation I'd got for a hundred and fifty bucks and it was running, but barely. As soon as I clocked out I wished I could just give up on Kurt. Or maybe I should have told Regina to call an ambulance. But he was real sick inside a meth lab, and they'd both get arrested.

I got to Regina's grandma's house around 2:30 in the morning. The house was lopsided, built way back in the late 1800s. After Regina's grandma died back in the 1970s, Regina had forgotten all about it—till she and Kurt started brainstorming about the meth lab.

The old white-washed house was surrounded by knotty trees and a creek and fields and nothing else. I ran past the candle-lit kitchen with the sink ripped out, the whole house smelling of cold animals. Regina wasn't even there. Kurt was inside a sleeping bag on the floor with a lit flashlight next to his head. He had some blood coming down his lips and his head was hot. The meth lab was situated mostly on an old ratty-looking pool table beside the sleeping bag: one big blue plastic vat and a couple propane tanks and six or seven gallons of ammonia and a bunch of plastic bags from Walgreens.

I carried Kurt to the car and got him into the emergency room at some small-town hospital on the Ohio/Indiana state-line. They took him back and asked if he had insurance and of course he didn't but they still took him as an indigent case, and I just sat out in the waiting room hoping he wouldn't die.

It turned out to be just plain old-fashioned double-pneumonia. Kurt hadn't eaten for a week and he was taking speed and not drinking anything but Red Bulls and vodka and finally he just dehydrated and the virus got into his system. He was in the hospital for ten days, on major antibiotics and oxygen.

I went to see him every day. Brought him magazines and at one point he requested a goddamn coloring book and crayons, which I brought to him too.

As Kurt got better he kept looking at me until one day, about a day before he was released, he said: "You saved my life, motherfucker."

He smiled and laughed a little and looked so beautiful in the hospital bed. Pale and fragile, he had longer hair then, curly, and glossy eyelids that he would shut for a long time as he talked. It was like he was enjoying his heavenly rehabilitation. Like he'd gotten sick on purpose to have this time alone with me. All I could do was deliver to him what he needed and wanted. We had the relationship I wanted, I realized.

"I guess I did."

The room was tiny. It had a crucifix above the bed and off to the side was a little bathroom with a metal faucet. His old clothes hung on the door hook. After getting out, he would be $26,000.00 in debt and would never be able to pay and would go bankrupt, but right then he was clean and pale, and he was looking at me with gratitude.

"I owe you, buddy."

I knew he would never love me back the way I wanted him to. He was giving me his complete attention there in the hospital, because he would need me to pick him up and take him home and help him buy meds. But eventually he would just leave me.

+

Kurt came home with me and he stayed for a month and then left. I didn't see him again until about two months ago, when I was at the Goodwill buying a winter coat. He looked exactly the same, except he had a skullcap because his hairline was receding. He told me he was working at a convenience store and that the woman next to him was his girlfriend, Elaine Roosevelt. She managed the Goodwill. Elaine smiled.

We started hanging out at Elaine's house, ordering pizzas and getting high and watching movies. Kurt told me he took pictures of Elaine and was thinking about starting his own porn website. I still wanted Kurt so bad even though I knew the whole thing was useless, and even though I had Jeremy. I was in the middle of them on the couch one night in Elaine's house and it was quiet except for Tom Cruise in *War of the Worlds* and Kurt told Elaine to kiss me.

4

Elaine's house is on B Street next to a house that says "for sale by owner" in spray-painted letters right on the aluminum siding. When I arrived for Super Bowl Sunday, I discovered a brand new flat-screen TV hanging on Elaine's wall and a new desk off to the side with a huge new Macintosh computer on it.

Elaine and Kurt are now in the kitchen. Enrique and Stephanie, Kurt and Elaine's friends, are sitting on the floor watching the pre-game show. Enrique doesn't speak English that well and he is wearing a red tee-shirt and jeans. Stephanie has stringy blonde hair and looks like she might be twelve years old. Enrique keeps touching and tickling her. He is a roofer, Kurt said, from Mexico City, and Stephanie is his fiancée. She lives in the projects with her grandma.

When I first arrived a few hours ago, Elaine was in the bathroom and wouldn't come out. But Kurt was real happy to see me. He was decked out in Indianapolis Colts gear, a jersey and matching jogging shorts and tennis shoes and cap. He had even painted his face like the fans do, one side blue and one side white.

"Come on in, friend," he said and I followed and he showed me the new TV and the computer Elaine got for him to help run his website. He told me about the credit-card company he had just hooked up with for the fees he was going to be charging. Then he took me into Elaine's basement and showed me a pot garden he was cultivating: plastic planters and fluorescent tubes and electrical stuff.

"It's all about making money now," Kurt said, his face shiny with the half-blue and half-white. "I'm not really into pot so I know I won't be smoking away my profits, you know?"

He laughed and coughed.

"Yeah," I said.

We stood there for a second in the basement. Kurt stepped over and he whispered into my face, almost like he was noticing what I was thinking:

"Elaine's suicidal again." He smiled. "In the bathroom being all suicidal." He rolled his eyes. "We're gonna have to work on her."

It seemed like he enjoyed saying that, like it was a poem he had written. Then Kurt kissed me on the mouth and some of the greasy face-paint got on my face and hair. I opened my mouth and we kissed more.

We went upstairs. He showed me the video of the three of us doing it on the website he was creating. It didn't look like what I thought it would, but I still couldn't watch it. The website was designed with Day-Glo colors and had a picture of Elaine in the logo part with her legs spread, her eyes lit up like a jack-o-lantern's. The website address was www.dontbeastranger.com. Coming out of Elaine's mouth was a cartoon bubble that read: "Don't be a stranger!!!"

Right when Kurt was getting ready to show me some more pictures on his site, Elaine came out dressed in her own Colts outfit, except she didn't have any face paint. She had puffy eyelids, but she was not crying.

She walked up to me and said: "Glad you could make it."

Kurt got up from the computer and turned the TV on.

"We gotta go make the chili, honey," he said.

"I know."

She noticed that I had some of Kurt's face paint on my face, and she smiled, but somehow look hurt and ragged, and I thought she was going to scratch me or hold onto me for dear life or maybe both. Then she walked on into the kitchen with Kurt. A second or two later the doorbell rang and Kurt told me to let in Enrique and Stephanie.

+

The game has just started. It's raining hard at the Super Bowl in Miami. Enrique is laughing loud and so is Kurt. The three of us are in the kitchen. Stephanie and Elaine are in the bathroom.

The blue and white paint on Kurt's face has smeared together like a sky and clouds. He's stirring the big pot of chili. Enrique is eating nachos. I go over and whisper to Kurt: "Isn't Steph a little too young?"

I laugh too. It's like that with Kurt—even though you know you're right you are embarrassed anyway.

"She's eighteen," he says, smiling real big.

Elaine comes into the room. She goes over to Kurt and knocks the big spoon out of the pot and his hand in one swoop, like she swung in from the ceiling.

"You are not taking pictures of that girl no more," she said. "She's in there in the bathroom bleeding. I'm sick of this."

Ten minutes ago, Kurt had shot some pictures of Enrique and Stephanie but that was upstairs while me and Elaine got stuff prepared. I cut up some carrots and green peppers and made ranch dip and she iced her brownies.

We were both quiet as hell, except at one point she came over and said how good I was doing, like a school teacher who is trying too hard to like a student she hates.

The spoon hits the floor and chili from it goes all over the place and onto Kurt's leg and he pretends he is a burn victim and tries to go after her Elaine. Finally she just says that she wants him out of her house.

"I've had it," she says.

Then there's a horrible quiet in the house, except for the football game.

Enrique stops eating and Stephanie's in the bathroom bleeding. Elaine screams real high-pitched.

She says, "I want you out of here!"

Then she starts beating on him. He laughs, and me and Enrique back out of the kitchen, and then Kurt comes out, saying "Fuck you, bitch."

She goes for his computer in the living room, and it's like Rocky with the TV. Elaine picks it up and smashes the screen onto the floor, then kicks the actual computer.

"I don't want no evidence of this," she says.

She keeps talking to herself, pulling the mouse out of the computer and taking it into the kitchen. I hear her dump it into the chili. Then she screams again.

I go to the door. Kurt comes out after me. Enrique just takes off down the sidewalk. It's cold. I try to avoid Kurt, but he gets into my car, laughing. I start it up.

"Man," he says. "I mean, I knew she was messed up, but damn..."

He laughs the way he always laughs, like he just robbed a bank and killed somebody and then forgot the money on the counter. I drive off and get on the interstate that will take us to my place. I feel sort of superior in a way, like he's chosen me, and yet that feeling melts away quick and I wind up feeling trapped again. He's going on about getting his halogen pot lights back and how it's no skin off his back if she trashes the computer—she bought it anyways. But there was a whole lot of damn work inside the computer for the website and who was she to judge him, she did the same stuff he did.

Kurt goes, "Man, I have got to pee."

He points at a rest area sign flying by.

"You got a heater in this thing?" he asks.

I drive on up to the rest area. Just a couple semis and a mini-van are out front. I park, and the lights inside the glassed-in shelter glow bright, with a picture of the governor of Ohio center-stage on a paneled wall. Kurt runs in. I stare at the governor's picture. Some old guy with jowls looking out at nothing, like he has all the answers but no one cares. The heater just keeps blowing cold air.

When I back out, I'm thinking I'll see Kurt in the rearview running toward my car. He'll be screaming for me to stop.

5

I knock on the door to Jeremy's apartment and he answers. He's in those sweats he wears, shocked to see me.

"Hey," he goes, and that's when I smell the cat piss. It's riding out from the door on a wave of furnace heat.

"Hey."

"What's up?"

We stand there until Jeremy laughs and tells me to come in. He has the Super Bowl on. It's still raining in Miami, and all the players are mud-covered. Jeremy grabs dirty clothes off the floor. There's a bag of Doritos over by the couch. When I knocked, I bet he was sacked out with his Big Gulp of Pepsi and chips, totally enjoying himself. I can just see it. But the cat-piss smell is raunchy and I feel nauseated.

Jeremy picks up a sweatshirt, and under it is one of the kittens. The orange one. It runs back down the small hallway to Jeremy's bedroom.

"I thought you took them to the shelter," I go.

The TV is real loud, so Jeremy turns it down.

"I tried," he says. He goes over to his little breakfast nook where he puts his laundry into a basket. Then he looks over at me. "I just couldn't. They were, like, screaming at me when I took them in. I pulled into the shelter parking lot out there on the bypass, and I got out, and I could hear them in my car. I looked into the box and the mom was dead and there they were with their dead mom, you know? And it's just, shit. I can't dump them off. I buried the mom out back and here we are."

Jeremy takes me to his bedroom. His bed is not made. The piss smell is really bad. I get down on my hands and knees to look under the bed. The kittens have set up their own little hiding place under the headboard. The orange one looks at me in the dark and lets out a hiss, while the two gray ones wrestle.

"They've pissed everywhere," he says. "I've got carpet cleaning stuff but it doesn't take the smell away. I set up a litter box for them but they don't care. There goes my deposit."

I get up because my knees start to hurt.

Jeremy goes, "Why are you here anyway?" He's got more dirty clothes picked up from his bedroom floor.

"Just wanted to drop by."

"I got to go put these in the machine downstairs," he says.

I hear the two kittens wrestling. They make a soft thump like someone politely knocking on a window.

+

The Super Bowl is almost over.

"Look at it rain," Jeremy says, sitting on a dinette chair, folding the clothes he washed.

We'd ordered a pizza and it was gone. I'm stretched out on his couch. The orange cat has made its way back out and is half-asleep on one of Jeremy's folded towels. The cat-piss smell comes and goes, carried by heat when the furnace kicks on.

Jeremy says, "You gonna stay here tonight?"

I just need some place where I'm not by myself, I want to say. I just need company, and I look over at Jeremy and he's staring at me. I know he loves me and I bet he knows I don't love him, but does that really matter? I need him. I want him to know that I will do what I can to make some love come out of that.

"If you let me," I say.

Jeremy is silent. He keeps folding clothes. I think he's happy.

God Knows Where

I

We get into Urgent Care a little after 6:00 PM. The place is all scuffed-up walls, plaid furniture, a Christmas tree on a table. My three-year-old nephew, Shawn, is barely able to walk, his ear is hurting him so bad. Misty, my older sister and Shawn's mom, sits down in a love seat with him next to a rack of *People* magazines. I sign us in, then flop down on the love seat arm next to Shawn.

There's a guy across from us, sitting next to a woman with short dark hair. The woman's eyes look glazed over from being in a lot of pain. She's in a purple nurse's aide's uniform, cradling her left arm and licking her lips. The guy has a beard, dark skin, brown eyes. He's going bald on top. He looks away and then every once in a while talks to her out of the side of his mouth like their visit here is a secret. Sometimes he looks at me.

Shawn crawls over and I slide down off the arm. You can tell how bad he's hurting from how hot he is.

Misty goes, "He loves you so much Andy," not drunk, just scared.

"I know."

I'm looking at the guy, making it seem like I am not by tilting my head toward Shawn.

The receptionist calls from the doorway, "Jeanetta Richmond."

The woman the guy is with gets up and walks toward the door. He gets up from his seat, and she turns around and goes, "Don't worry about it. Just wait on me."

Then she says "damn" under her breath. He sits back down.

Shawn is twitchy in my lap from his pain. Misty gets her cell phone out and calls her work to say she won't make it that night. She folds the thing back up and slides it into her purse.

"Fired," she goes.

Shawn starts to whimper, and I kiss the top of his head. I see the guy looking back at me. Then out of nowhere he's smiling at me weird.

"My fucking child is sick, and I'm fired." She says that loud enough for anyone to hear. Laughs too. She'd just got the job two weeks ago—Bob Evans—so it's not a big tragedy, but I'm sure she is going to use this new development as yet another reason to have a meltdown either here or once she gets home or maybe both.

The guy across from us goes, "Cute kid."

To me. His voice is low and growly. Misty looks at him, then at Shawn and me.

"He's mine," she goes, putting her hand on Shawn's back, and Shawn buries his head in my neck.

"My nephew," I go.

The receptionist calls Shawn's name. Misty picks him up, tells me she can handle this part. The guy is smiling at me still.

"You smoke?" he goes.

I nod my head. He bums a cigarette off me and we go outside. It's spitting snow. His name turns out to be Doug. He takes the smoke in hard and it doesn't seem to come back out, like he swallows instead of inhales.

"My girlfriend hurt her shoulder at work," Doug says. "We both work at Careview Nursing Home, on Mason Road."

A semi goes past. This particular Urgent Care is right across the street from Big Lots, Wendy's and a dry-cleaning place. The semi splashes gray snow all over some dead-looking bushes out front. After it takes off you can hear the boxed-in voice of the Wendy's drive-thru. A fat lady in a sweatsuit marches toward us from her Dodge Omni. We have to go to the side of the front door to continue smoking. The sidewalk drops off, so we get closer to talk.

"Rough week, man," Doug says.

"Yeah, me too."

"I mean, really rough." He looks around, eyes going into slits. "I work on the Alzheimer's unit at Careview, right? You know, it's locked down and there's people in there don't know what a fucking *door* is and just kind of say gobbledygook all the time and walk off, slobber and crap everywhere. And, like okay, I was mopping the front foyer before my shift ended couple days ago. I was mopping, and I got the front door to the foyer propped open, and I guess this one really bad Alzheimer guy, Mr. Carpenter, skinny little guy, I guess he got out when I was changing the mop water. They had to call the cops and everything. He got out around 2:00 AM, I guess. It's been on the damn TV news. You seen it?"

He looks afraid, like he might be lying, but why the hell would he lie about something like that?

"No. I don't have a TV."

He smiles big, goes on.

"I mean, okay, I left the door open, but the dude would have to walk past like two nurse's stations and shit, which he did, so it's really all our faults."

He puts the cigarette out on the sidewalk, looks at me like he wants something, then laughs at himself.

"Got another one?"

I give it to him.

"Sucks," he says, lighting up. "I'm on administrative leave, whatever the hell that means. The fucking RN there is talking criminal neglect charges. But you know what's worse?"

"What?"

"Mr. Carpenter, you know, out there, God knows where."

That's a lot to deal with, I want to say, but I just smoke and think about how I would like to kiss Doug on the mouth.

"Oh yeah—she'll kick me out. I mean, Jeanetta, my girlfriend. I mean she's the greatest person on earth, man. She helped me turn my whole damn life around, but I have fucked up so many times."

I don't know what else to say, so I go: "I just moved into a new apartment."

"Where?"

"Winter Flower Estates over on Route Six."

"Wow. I saw them going up." He takes another long drag, then puts his cigarette out and goes, "We're freezing our balls off out here."

The waiting room is empty now except for the fat lady. She's crocheting. On the TV are a man and a woman holding hands in support of a cock-stiffening pill. We sit down next to each other over by the magazine rack. Someone has plugged in the Christmas tree. The lights blink. We both give off that cold dirty-chimney smell from smoking outside.

"Hey, you know what?" Doug says.

"What?"

"Three-fifty is totally what I could afford. You mind if I come over and take a look at yours? Have a tour?" He looks at me all fake and happy, and I just can't look away.

"Sure."

"What's your number?" He whispers that.

"Phone isn't hooked up yet. I had a cell phone but it was just too fucking expensive."

"Well, you call me then. Tomorrow. Okay? Let me know when I can come over to check it out?"

I go up and ask for a piece of scrap paper and a pen. Doug writes down his number just as Jeanetta comes out.

"Thank God they take workers' comp," she says to nobody in particular.

The fat lady stops crocheting, nods her head real serious. Jeanetta just walks past Doug, who stands up and whispers at me, "Don't forget."

2

Four years ago I lived on 12th Street in a garage behind an old lady's house, right off downtown. The back space of this garage had been partitioned off and turned into a little apartment for her son, who was retarded, but then he died of cancer and so she rented it out to me. It was painted sky blue inside and had vinyl furniture because I think the man must have peed himself a lot. There was a sunflower wall clock and a small fridge and hot plate and kitchen table from the forties. It always smelled like exhaust and old rubber. But seventy-five a month.

Four years ago, too, my dad offered to pay for my first year at the community college. I did not trust him, had no reason to, but he said he wanted to pay, like a peace offering for all the other shit he'd pulled. So I said okay. Just to be sure, though, I asked him to show me the receipt once he paid. He did, and it looked completely legit. So I went to English 120 and zoology and sociology and was making good grades. I was thinking about being a paralegal or something. Then one day, toward the end of the semester, a lady from the bursar's office came and got me in English class and tells me I owe for the whole semester.

I called Dad. He was not at work. Called him at home, and he was not there.

I owed twenty-three hundred bucks. If I didn't pay it by the next day, I would be shit out of luck. Which meant everything I did to make good grades, the papers I wrote, the questions I answered, the books I read, all just got flushed down the toilet.

Turns out my dad was back to gambling. He was crazy-eyed when I met him at Squeezer's, some skank bar he frequented—big-bellied, small-headed, mustached, leather-coated. I sat down next to him, and he was all smiles.

"What you want, Andy? Beer?"

I wanted to kill him, it hurt so much. I mean, I cried right there at the bar. He confessed and even told me how he'd used some receipt book he got at Office Depot to make the receipt he'd showed me. He told me he really wanted to make me happy, even if it was a big lie. He told me he'd get a loan at the bank tomorrow to cover the tuition. But finally I had the reason to tell him: "I fucking hate you."

I was still crying kind of.

"Join the club," he said.

"Fuck you."

I left.

That was that.

I started working more hours at the United Dairy Farmers, a convenience store near downtown, telling myself I would save up enough to go back to school next fall. Mostly I worked nights. I didn't have a car. After clocking out at 2:00 AM, I would put on my Walkman and walk home: long walks through downtown, where all the buildings were so vacated it looked like they were underwater.

Then one night, a couple months after Dad fucked me over, I was walking beside this park on D Street, surrounded by all these houses built too close together, some abandoned and half-rotten, bending over toward the street. I was just walking and listening to Incubus, making myself go deaf. I didn't even feel the first punch or kick.

Two guys. Didn't see them. After I felt the second or third wallop, I heard one guy say, "You out here looking for some dick, fag?"

I really wasn't. I didn't even know this was where you went if you were a fag. I mean, I knew of course I was a fag, but I didn't know what I was supposed to be doing. It wasn't in my blood. I was just some dumb-ass walking home from work.

They beat the living shit out of me, used some piece of something—I don't know, maybe a hammer. I couldn't see much. I saw them like you see dogs barking in a rearview mirror. They finally stopped. Some lady driving home from her night shift saw me and called the cops. Broken clavicle. Bruises all over. No internal organs damaged that bad though. I was in the hospital for three days.

Dad came to the hospital with Misty. They brought me some flowers and a Stephen King book. Dad looked apologetic.

"They get your wallet?" he said.

"No."

Here he was trying to be Super Dad again.

Misty always helped him out, always forgave him. At the time, she was pregnant with Shawn but didn't know it. She was partying like it was 1999 (which it was, actually), sometimes crashing at my place, but mostly living at other people's places, like Dad's crappy trailer.

Misty said, "No, Daddy. He was gay bashed. It was a hate crime."

She burst into tears. My dad just looked away. I knew what he was thinking—that he was glad he'd fucked up the money for my school, that I deserved not having it, being what I was.

"I'm so sorry, buddy," he said, bending down to me. He was crying a little, but he always did that shit.

"Just leave me the fuck alone," I said. I had hit rock bottom. I was gay bashed, but I didn't even have a fucking boyfriend or nothing.

Misty stopped crying and went, "Andy, come on. He's your Dad." She had short spiky bleached-out hair back then.

I glared at her and tried to roll over so I would not have to look at him, and he said, "I guess I can take a hint." He laughed under his breath and took off.

Misty bitched, but I didn't care.

I haven't talked to Dad since that day. He went back to Tennessee where he grew up, according to Misty, to work at a tire factory. Mom told me she thought he was living with his mom. My mom has a good job up in Toledo working for an insurance company, and she's got a husband and they're doing okay, but she never had enough to pay for my college or nothing. And anyway I never went back to school. Went full time at the convenience store. Wound up moving in with Misty once she had Shawn, helped her out with him for a while. Got lead clerk (not management—gotta have a degree even at a fucking convenience store), made a little more money, got a car, finally decided to move out on my own.

And there you have it: my life.

3

After we leave Urgent Care, me and Misty and Shawn go to Walgreens to get Shawn's antibiotic, which costs one hundred twenty-four bucks. I don't mind, I keep saying, and Misty keeps saying she will pay me back. I also get Shawn some coloring stuff. We drive back to Misty's place, where we find her boyfriend in the shadows, watching *Survivor*. The place smells like chili and old water. I carry Shawn, and Misty flicks on the light. Chuck is the boyfriend's name, and he opens his eyes wide. He has the top of his Arby's uniform on, and below that just underwear and socks.

"What time is it?" Chuck says.

"8:30," Misty goes. "I got fired."

"I told you."

"Shut up," Misty says, putting the prescriptions on the breakfast bar next to an open box of Little Debbie's.

Shawn's still hot and he's growling like sick kids do. When I lived here, I couldn't stand Chuck and Misty sitting around, making up schemes, bossing one another around, but not moving. I put Shawn in his room, which I helped him decorate: dark blue walls with star decals and a Buzz Lightyear lamp.

God Knows Where

I kiss him on the head, and his eyes open all of sudden. He looks like he could smile. But just says, "Me."

"What?"

Shawn wraps his arms around my neck, pushing his head into my collarbone. I can feel his heat of his fever, and he moans real quiet. I sit back with him and let him nuzzle into me like that, like he is trying to find a way out of what is hurting him through pushing into me.

When I go back out to the living room, Chuck's telling Misty to turn off the goddamn lights. He hates watching TV with the lights on. Misty says she's trying to get Shawn's medicine ready.

Chuck just grunts and goes, "Oh, yeah—your dad called."

"When? Why didn't he call me on my cell?" Misty gets up from the dinette table with the bottle of pills.

"He lost your cell number."

"What did he say?"

"Call him. Fucking call him!"

Chuck just got the job at Arby's but usually hangs out with people who make meth and go to strip clubs and hunt.

"Shit... Andy—can you take Shawn his medicine?"

Looking at her ratty hair and her round, plump face, I remember when we rode the school bus together. Nobody liked her really, and I'd be there trying to make it look like I was above her. But there was guilt by association. We were trash anyway so it wasn't like I had some reputation to uphold.

I take Shawn his medicine. He puts the spoon into his mouth without one word, like he was born to take medicine. I go back out into the living room and as I'm passing there's a news brief about that Mr. Carpenter. The lady anchor with blonde hair and big red lips is telling the local community that Mr. Carpenter has still not been found and that, with the temperatures being what they are, he could be frostbitten or worse. Then there's his daughter or somebody in tears. I don't say anything.

Misty's on her cell with Dad. She's whispering but then she sees me and goes, "You want to talk to him?"

"No."

Chuck gets up and goes into the kitchen. He opens the freezer and then it's like a bomb going off. He's using Misty's messed-up blender to make himself a milkshake.

Misty goes, "I'm sorry, Dad... Chuck! Goddammit! What are you fucking doing?"

+

That next day, I call Doug from work. It's 2:00 in the afternoon, and I just spent the last sixteen hours at the store because someone called off. Calling him is my reward for not having gone completely nuts. A new girl named Darla has come in to relieve me. I should stay to train her, but I am over it. Tomorrow I'm off. I don't care.

I pull out from the parking lot, poor old Darla in there looking scared. The building itself is all plate-glass windows covered in cigarette and milkshake posters faded from direct sunlight.

When I get to Winter Flower Estates, I see Doug waiting in front of my building.

"Hey," he says, so happy to see me it's got to be a put-on.

"Wow. You got here before I did," I go.

"I just came on over soon as you called."

"Yeah, I see."

We go on into my apartment, and as soon as I open my door and he walks in, he whistles like he's truly impressed.

"You're kidding me. Three fifty? No way man."

He walks into the bathroom and then through the kitchenette. He has on jeans and a Guns N' Roses tee-shirt and boots and a corduroy jacket. His hair is a little oily. He shaved his beard off so he looks like he's fourteen.

"Yup, three fifty."

I have nothing really, except a bed and a couch I got at Goodwill the other day. The couch is brown and clean-looking. Doug comes up to me. His breath smells bad but that's okay.

"Well, it's official," he says.

"What?"

"Jeanetta kicked me out."

His smile gets brighter. He laughs. Then puts on the brakes.

"You hungry?" he says.

"Sure."

We take his car to this McDonald's, a mile down the interstate. He orders two Quarter Pounders, fries and a shake, and I get a fish sandwich and a Coke. In a newspaper left over from breakfast, Doug finds the story of old man Carpenter. There's a picture that makes him look like the dude who hates Christmas in that Christmas movie.

Doug goes: "Listen. 'Carpenter's family says it is contemplating legal action against Careview, Inc., the company that owns the facility where he was living.' Shit." He puts the paper down and takes a big bite of his other sandwich and swallows. There's a mildew smell mixed with the hot vapor of French fries. It's spitting snow outside again.

Doug looks at me, as he chews. He swallows and goes: "We used to do threesomes." His grin turns into a serious straight line. He's whispering. "Me and Jeanetta and this other guy from the nursing home who worked in dietary. We did threesomes, but it didn't work out. Jerry, the guy, he got jealous of me and started calling us up and stuff."

I finish my sandwich.

"Mr. Carpenter," Doug goes, saying the name out loud just because he had to.

+

Doug drives us back to my apartment. When he pulls in, I see Chuck and Misty and Shawn getting out of Chuck's vehicle, a Chevy Malibu the color of Halloween. Chuck has on his full Arby's uniform this time. Shawn has a huge piece of cotton in his ear. Misty is in a dark blue dress and high heels.

I go over. Misty is all pissed.

"Well, guess what?" she says. "Dad's dying."

Shawn comes over and hugs my leg, jumps up into my arms. He feels a little hot, but he doesn't seem as sick as last night. It's forty degrees, and he doesn't have a fucking coat on, like the cotton in his ear is all the protection he needs.

Chuck laughs. "I told her you wouldn't care."

Doug is over by the door to my complex, just standing, and that's when Misty sees him, and goes, almost smiling, "Is that that guy from Urgent Care last night?"

I nod, and Shawn goes, "Grandpa's gonna die."

"What's he doing with you?" Misty says. "I thought he was with that woman."

Chuck goes, "Look, I'll drive you to the bus station, but we got to leave now, girl. I got to be in at work at 5:30."

Chuck is all career-minded now that Misty needs him to take her to the bus station. I flash on Dad's face in my head, the one he wore telling jokes during the holidays, when we had the money for holidays, how he was all red-complected and full of life, eyes blazing with the joy he could bring to people. Then I flash on him curled up on a barstool, watching a college football game he had put a thousand on, afraid and thrilled and full of life in a different way, like he wanted to make a big mistake so he could come down really hard and lose everything he had to live for and still be alive.

Misty comes over, "Is he your boyfriend?" It comes out real mean.

Like I've ever had a boyfriend! Once or twice, almost boyfriends, guys from the store. One time I went to a bar in Dayton and met someone, but then it turned he was schizo and tried to steal my car.

I just go, "You better get going."

Then Misty's pissed. "He is your dad and he is dying!"

"I'm sorry about that," I say. I kind of like being calm right then, with Shawn in my arms, tucking his head down.

"I better get him inside. Where's his coat?"

Chuck goes, opening his car door, "Won't wear it, little son of a bitch." He laughs and gets Shawn's parka out and gives it to me. Misty looks at Doug.

"You ought to go with me and forgive him on his death bed," she says, and that's when I get that she's bad-drunk. She has it all worked out, how me and him will reunite and all will be fine with the world.

"What's he dying of?"

"I don't know," she says, and then she closes her eyes dramatically. It's like she wants to turn into a statue, all drunk and dressed up on the way to her dad's death bed. I'm sorry for her. Holding onto Shawn, I walk toward where I live.

Chuck goes, "Can you take care of him tomorrow too?"

"Yeah, sure."

He starts his car and Misty unfreezes herself.

"You fucking fag!" she yells. "You little faggot!" Then she hollers out a drunk sob, and goes, "I'm sorry! You're just pissing me off!"

I keep walking.

4

That night, we go to the Dollar General Store. Me and Doug and Shawn buy stuff for my place: towels, a white plastic dish drainer, a bathroom toilet brush, and a little plastic carrier for bathroom cleaner and Windex and paper towels. Shawn is doing better. He's in his coat, walking around kind of stunned and cranky, but still interested in getting a toy. The lights in Dollar General are so bright it makes you feel like you're on board a spaceship.

Doug asks one of the cashiers if they sell TVs.

A scrawny-looking black lady in a yellow smock goes, "No."

"You need a TV," he says.

"I know," I say.

"I don't know how you live without TV."

Shawn comes over with an action figure, some mutant dragon-man. It's only three dollars.

"Sure," I say.

The cotton in his ear makes him look like a poor lost orphan. I tuck it in, and he jerks his head away. Then I look up and I can see me and Doug and Shawn in the plate-glass windows, which create a perfect mirror because it's so dark out and it's so bright inside. Me in jeans and my winter coat, holding onto the towels and dish drainer, and Doug in his Guns N' Roses tee, holding onto the cleaners and toilet brush, and Shawn in his parka, holding his toy.

Then there's this second of time when I can feel myself going into the reflection, like I am leaving everything behind and turning into a vision of what I think the future might be.

Doug says, "Hey, Andy, do you got a toaster?"

+

Back home, I put the dish drainer next to the sink, the towels on the rack in the bathroom, all the cleaners and toilet brush in the closet in the hall. After I give him his medicine, Shawn just lies on the couch with the mutant-thing on his chest.

Doug whispers, "I'm going over to Jeanetta's for some stuff."

We're in the kitchen.

"Okay."

We kiss right there, my eyes closed. When I open them, Shawn's looking at us, then away. I take in Doug's smell. Cigarettes and Right Guard and stinky breath covered up with cinnamon gum. I want to collapse into it, like when I was a kid and I'd climb up on a dresser and dive headfirst into a pile of dirty clothes.

"Bye, Shawn," Doug says going past, out the door.

I go into the living room. There's an old clock radio that doesn't tell time anymore and only gets three stations. It's on the floor. I flick it on to Lite Rock 98. Heart, singing some slow song.

I lie down on the couch next to Shawn, and he says, "He's dumb."

"Who?"

"That guy," he says.

"Oh, he's all right."

I laugh, and Shawn curls up on me, kind of painful at first, elbow in my ribs, and then the action figure drops to the floor. Me and Shawn go to sleep.

I wake up when Doug comes back a few hours later. He's got a box of stuff and a duffel bag. We didn't even talk about him moving in, but I don't care. After McDonald's, we tongue-kissed in his car without saying nothing, there in the parking lot. I keep thinking about what love does to you when you don't let yourself know you need it. You have to keep thinking you don't need it so you won't lose your mind.

I pick Shawn up. He's all deadweight. Carry him into my bedroom and tuck him in.

Doug is unpacking in the kitchen.

"I got this toaster when I first moved in with Jeanetta." He laughs. "I am a Pop-Tart-aholic."

On the radio is a one song by Mariah Carey I used to hate but I like now. After he's done unpacking in the kitchen he comes out. We both get naked. He's skinny and kind of hairy, with that stupid face that makes my heart claw at itself, like my heart's got fleas. He whispers, asking me if I got any hand lotion or something like that and I don't.

He goes, "Hey, that's okay. We'll do what we can with what we got"

He laughs at his remark, like he is and always will be his own built-in audience.

We start kissing, and then we get down on the floor. I can tell he likes what I am doing to him, each touch, lick, and bite. We laugh sometimes. He loves me back like he loves anybody else, quick grunts and long pauses. He kisses my neck and tells me while his mouth is still against my skin that I am what he has needed all this time.

5

The radio is still on the next morning. Doug's already up and in the bathroom taking a shower. The Dave and Carrie Morning Show is playing. I stay on the floor in my underwear, looking up at the ceiling. Then after an Air Supply song a lady says it's time for the news. The top story is that the elderly man with Alzheimer's who walked away from a nursing facility late last week has been found. His body was located behind a Circuit City in some weeds three miles from Careview Nursing Home, the lady says. Authorities say he died from exposure.

The lady goes on, but I get up and turn off the radio, real quiet. I stand outside the bathroom door with the shower going, the smell of hot soap turning into lather. I feel like I could stand there for the rest of my life.

Doug is dressed and he's in the kitchen, making Pop-Tarts. I walk in. He looks so goddamn happy. They're blueberry. He's in a brown sweater and tan corduroy pants, white socks, hair still damp.

"Hey," he says. He pushes the lever down on the toaster.

"Sleep good?" I say.

"Oh yeah." He laughs and looks away, waiting for the Pop-Tarts, and then he goes, "I'm gonna go check the paper to see the news. Anything on the radio?"

I could tell him, but I don't.

"No. Just the regular old bullshit."

I'm glad I don't have a TV. Or a phone. And fuck the radio too. I realize this apartment here is the perfect place to be if you don't want to be anywhere else. The Pop-Tarts pop up then. Doug claps his hands like a little kid, like he won't be able to let them cool down before he eats one.

"Don't look so sad," he says to me. "Pop-Tarts, motherfucker. Pop. Tarts."

Then we eat some and he kisses me and he leaves.

I go into the bedroom, where Shawn is. As I lean down to him I can see his sweat has soaked the pillow. His dark blonde hair is darker from the wet. His mouth is wide open, like he's laughing and not laughing at the same time. Some dream maybe where he is the only one who gets the joke.

How to Get from This to This

I

My brother, Lucas, leaves a message on my answering machine.

"I am out here in my car on my cell phone, Danny, and I swear to God you better not be in there hiding. They've towed your car. Are you drinking? Call me. We love you."

One time I caught him and his high-school boyfriend out in the tree house he and I had built. I climbed up to smoke a joint. They were hot and heavy, and he looked so happy and helpless on top of his sleeping bag. His face was extremely alive.

I just had to say something.

"They can hear you guys in the house," I said.

Lucas got up real quick, terrified, and the boy who had been joyfully sucking him off jumped up like he'd been electrocuted.

"I mean, quiet down." I laughed under my breath, trying to seem cool.

Lucas, sixteen and full of venom because he was caught, goes, "Get out!"

From then on it was like he was superior to me because I had caught him. Even though I said not one thing to anyone, still he had that superior attitude, like at any moment I would go stool pigeon on him and he would have to defend cocksucking at a family reunion. Which he kind of had to do eventually anyway when he brought his college butt-buddy home with him. He was real serious about how much he loved the guy and how nothing would change that, not his parents or God or anybody.

2

A few months back, in the ironed jeans and fresh crisp blouse she wears to work, Jill said: "Do you think you are the only one who sees how fucked up and shitty everything is?"

"Watch the language," I said, lighting up a joint.

I am thirty-three years old and she's twenty-four and we met in a community college English class when I was still trying to get my degree in whatever. At that time, I think it was computer graphics.

Standing by the bed, she said, "Give me a toke." She took in the smoke and walked backwards a little, bumping into the treadmill Lucas had given me for Christmas. She's got short blonde hair, and she goes to a tanning booth, but not to get extra crispy, just healthy. She was so beautiful I wanted her to leave most of the time.

I got up and went to the bathroom. This was when I was not drinking, when I maybe had a chance at management at Applebee's Neighborhood Bar and Grill. I was helping to open a brand-spanking-new location out by the overpass. I was that good.

I came out of the bathroom, smiling.

Jill noticed the look in my eyes and said, "Oh shit," kind of laughing.

When I kissed her, she liked it, I could tell. It is so goddamn mysterious how she could give herself up to me knowing what she did, how weak I was. But right then I was strong, I guess. When I pushed her onto the mattress on the floor, she yelled and laughed. We did it even though she had just gotten ready for work.

3

I finish the bottle around 6:00 PM and go outside. It's August, and the hot wind smells from the shit-filled river by the water-treatment plant. The apartment complex parking lot is filled with just-bought used cars. A big dumpster sits nearby like some fat pissed-off robot waiting to eat what's left.

I start walking at the side of the road in my 1982 Rush tee and jeans and no-sock Converses. Cars pass by. No one seems to see me. I trudge through some ditch slime, past a big diamond-shaped church, past the half-built Wal-Mart, past a neighborhood of brand-new cardboard houses, under a huge water tower and then into the little town, which is drowsy and abandoned. Being fucked-up in the dark, I feel like I'm a little kid wandering through a carnival in my pajamas.

At Mutt's Sports Bar, I order myself a Jack and Coke. As I take some money out of my pocket, I say to the bartender, "I wish you guys took coupons."

He doesn't even laugh, just gets the drink. It's not that crowded. The four-man country-rock band plays "Sweet Home Alabama" followed by "Cuts Like a Knife." I gulp and wonder what time it is, and then the bartender goes, "It's for you."

I take the receiver.

"I am out in the parking lot right now," Lucas says.

"Mutt's parking lot?"

"Yes."

"Jesus, Lucas." I laugh. It feels like there's bubbles in my bloodstream, like there's an old worn out game of Pac-Man going on inside my veins.

"I am going to come in there and kick your ass," Lucas says.

We both laugh.

"How's Craig?" That's his boyfriend.

"Fine… Come on, Dan. Jesus. You can't keep doing this. They towed your car. What the hell are you going to do without a car? Aren't you supposed to be working?"

I am shocked at how Lucas never gets it.

I give the receiver back to the bartender, and he goes, "There's a pay phone outside."

"I'm done with phone calls."

"If he calls you again, I'm telling him to call you on the pay phone."

"Fine."

How to Get from This to This

I realize this must happen a lot, my brother calling me at Mutt's. I always come here, like my life's journey is on a loop tape. But every time I come, I don't remember it.

Right then, the Wayne Man makes his nightly appearance. He is tall and gangly and mentally retarded, wearing a tee-shirt and work pants and flip-flops. His three-wheel bicycle is out there on the sidewalk.

The bartender goes, "Wayne, we're closing."

"I know. I know. I just wanted to come in and say hi."

Wayne's got greasy hair. He's overweight, and his voice is low-pitched and dull and prissy. He has bad acne. When he talks, he spits a little. The people left at the bar back away from him instinctively, like he's a really sick animal that just got in through a window

I am almost out of it, about to sink properly into a sinkhole. Wayne comes over.

"Hey, Danny," he says.

"Hey, Wayne."

"How's it going, bud?" He sits down next to me on a stool, smelling pretty ripe. Everything is so blurry it feels like I am inside a car that is going through a car wash really slow.

"You seen the *Spider-Man* sequel yet?"

"Not yet."

"It's great." His eyes are all afire due to the movie. I notice people are leaving. I feel frozen next to Wayne.

"It's really great," he says.

Lucas comes in. He is in shorts and a tee-shirt and sockless canvas shoes. He looks like Michael Douglas with his perfect combed-back hair. I'm proud of my brother with his slicked-back hair and his great job and his condo. He'll probably adopt some kid from China with his boyfriend. One time Lucas got beat up at school, and I remember how my mom wanted to help clean up his face, but he scowled at her and said, "This is mine." He was pointing at the bruises and the blood on his face.

Lucas comes over and whispers, "I'm taking you to my place."

I laugh. I am not ashamed to be handled like a bad-boy movie star being escorted by his manager. It's kind of touching. I smile. I want to take everything about myself and give it over to him in a little wrapped-up box with a letter that says, "Lucas, I love you." But it ain't that easy.

"I'm staying," I say.

Wayne says, "He's staying."

Two buds, me and Wayne. But Lucas is stubborn. He has glassy eyes from trying to hide his disgust, and I see from his point of view. Me—skinny, pale, thin-lipped, in a 1982 Rush tee, with no job or car, about to be evicted—sidled up in a bar next to some flannel-shirted moron with major zits. Not a pretty picture.

All of a sudden I get real mad.

"I'm fucking staying!" I scream. I swing my arms at Lucas, trying to hit him.

Lucas backs up. There's not a sound in the whole place. The band has stopped playing and is quietly packing up its gear. Lucas glares. I swing at him like I am trying to kill his face, and even though I love the faggot I can't take much more. I want the freedom of everybody hating me. The only true right a real full-blooded alkie has in this country is the right to get rid of everybody.

Lucas says, "Fuck you."

"Fuck you," Wayne says. He's got my back.

"Get out of here!" I yell in a mumbled bark, like a cartoon dog. I like this sudden exposure, this embarrassment. It fills me up with heat and sparks. Even the regret, as it starts to flood in, makes me happy that I've done what I've done: something final and real. Something that maybe will change my life.

Lucas has tears in his eyes.

"This is it, my man," he says, trying to sound all masculine. "Everybody is tired of you."

I feel so sorry for the guy, even though I'd like to hit him. I try to get back on my stool, turning my back on Lucas, but then I fall to the floor. Wayne helps me up, and I get a whiff of his piss stains and sweat.

The bartender comes out from behind the bar.

"Get up," he says. "Get up and get the fuck out of here."

I stand, thinking Lucas is still behind me. When I turn around and he's not, I tell myself, *See? See how much the fucker loves you?*

4

It is me and Wayne against the world. He helps me into the big wire basket on the back of his three-wheel bicycle. There's an orange August moon. As

Wayne pedals the bicycle up a hill and talks and talks and talks, I want to puke. But I hold it back.

Wayne knows where I live. When we get there, he parks his bike in front and chains it up.

"Can I see your comic book collection?" he says, sweat rolling off his nose.

I get out of the big basket and stand. The world is a bent piece of cardboard. I feel so dead I might as well be going up to people and screaming "boo." We walk up to my studio apartment, which I did not lock. Wayne makes himself right at home. He knows the routine. I see my apartment the way it truly is: mouse-bit bag of bread, Old Crow bottles, old textbooks I never sold back to the college bookstore. The magical couch with no cushions. What the fuck did I do with them?

Wayne lies down on my mattress after grabbing six or seven of my comic books, which I keep in big cardboard boxes beside the bathroom. I have collected them since I was nine years old. There's a fortune in those boxes. *Justice League of America, Number 12. Black Lightning, number 6. Green Lantern, number 21.*

Wayne takes off his shirt, lies back, and I flop down beside him.

"I wish I had this one," he whispers in awe.

I look over at the comic in his hands. His fingernails are painted black. On the yellowed page is a beautiful rendering of a woman turning into a laser-beam butterfly. On the next page is an ad for a miracle herbal supplement. There's a geek next to a bodybuilder and under the picture are the words: HOW TO GET FROM THIS TO THIS.

"That is beautiful," I whisper.

Wayne kisses me.

"I love you," he says.

"Thank you."

He kisses me again, and I can taste myself through him. He awkwardly pushes aside the comic books and yanks off his work pants. Naked, he looks like a white barrel-chested amoeba. I smile, drunk and stupefied. There is a reason I am on this earth, I'm thinking, as the boy goes down on me. Then in my head I see Jill and laser-beam butterflies and tanning booths and Frappuccinos. I remember the message she left me on my machine about six days ago: "Danny, don't do it anymore. Jesus fucking Christ."

I fall into the sleep I always sleep as Wayne does whatever else he wants to me. It's kind of like being attacked by an invisible dog. Wayne is the dude you see and run away from: the mental case you shield your children's eyes from, the reason neighbors sign petitions. But tonight he's in my dreams with me. The Wayne Man and me on a gondola in Venice, right?

5

Jill and I drove to a Ruby Tuesday's in the mall a few months back. I had a Diet Coke and a hamburger. She ate a third of her Caesar salad with grilled chicken.

"You look healthy," she said.

"I feel good."

She smiled. Despite all the other times I looked like a zombie, there I was in my plaid shirt and khakis, clean and sober, only smoking pot, still spilling out my sad-sack bullshit, but working and making plans and thinking about the future. I mean, soon enough, I'd be at Applebee's, inside its empty half-decorated shell, teaching new hires how to make nachos. You know: believing in myself. There were definite reasons for making a regular paycheck, like taking Jill out to eat and/or buying her perfume at Lazarus and/or thinking about buying a shiny blue used Honda Civic I'd seen in a dealer's lot.

After I paid, Jill and I stepped into the cold-cinnamon-android air of the mall. I loved her very deeply because right then it was so easy to do.

"Walk me to work," she whispered.

We held hands up the escalator at the Tri-County Mall, then walked past all the stores, so clean and still, past other couples, families, screaming babies. It was like I was delivering her to her savior. When we arrived at the Gap and stood beside the huge photos of half-smiling guys and gals in crisp casual clothes, I felt like we could be them: models without names, worth photographing, leading the good life.

We kissed goodbye. I swear to God I really wanted to tell her something good about the world, but she walked into the store and I walked out to the parking lot.

My fucking piece-of-shit car would not start.

At that moment, there was an avalanche on my home planet. Thoughts streaked through my head: *Green Lantern*, Old Crow, closed curtains and the smell of an empty can of Pringles. People probably think you just fall into that stuff, like tripping. But you have to make plans. I wanted a whole bottle poured directly into my brain, not through my mouth, but through a *Matrix*-like portal. I was living in a world where you could go from air-conditioned cinnamon smell and shiny new clothes to the cough and coma of a dead car in three seconds.

I called up Lucas, and he came to give me a jump. He was nervous because he knew what shit like this could do to me. He was being real helpful. My Ford Taurus came back to life in no time.

"That was easy," Lucas said. He unhooked the jumper cables like it was a little dance. "Nothing to it."

"Thanks," I said. But I hated him so much my teeth felt like they were rotting from it.

"How's Jill?" he asked, outside the driver's side window. I kept revving the engine.

"Fine."

"Great."

He was smiling. I just pulled out without saying goodbye, like it was his fault he had came here and saved me.

6

It's about 10:00 AM when I wake up. Wayne's snoring and naked. My head is so heavy I have to let it slide back to the mattress. I lie there, trying not to breathe, listening to Wayne.

Eventually he gets up, yawns. He stands and slides on his dirty underwear.

"You got any hot chocolate?" he says.

"No."

Then there is a knock on the door. A pounding. I pull Wayne back down onto the mattress and put my hand over his mouth. We stay like that while the pounding continues. I hear Jill. She says something that I am not going to write down.

7

Wayne is loading up what he can. He carries down a plastic grocery sack full of issues of *Green Lantern* and puts it carefully into the basket on his bike. He looks almost cross-eyed.

"You're sure about this?" he asks me later as he picks out more in my apartment.

I go over to my closet. "What size you wear?"

"Extra large."

"I think I have a few extra large tee-shirts. Maybe this jacket?"

He comes over and I put it on him like a butler. He struts for a second, excited about getting more stuff.

"Yeah, it fits," he says, almost proud. He can't zip the thing, but that's okay. This motherfucker is a survivor. I go in the kitchen and empty out my cabinets. He takes a box of mac-and-cheese and some cans of pork-n-beans. And last of all, an old model of a *Star Wars* TIE-fighter that was decorating my window sill. I help him carry stuff down until his bike basket is overloaded.

I feel superior to Wayne, like me giving him everything is a big joke, like he doesn't know I would throw it all in the dumpster anyway. But still it's like a gift. I don't even get choked up or morbid or anything.

We shake hands out in the parking lot and the sun gets in my eyes as it glitters on some tree limbs. I watch him get on his bike.

"Thanks, Dan," he says in a deep pitch.

He starts pedaling away, wheels crunching over the rock and pavement. It's a soft, sweet sound, like someone eating cereal.

I go back up to my apartment. The absence of the missing stuff is like a phantom pain. I catalog items in my head. Then I sit down on the mattress. Eventually I'll just get absorbed into what I've given the Wayne Man. I will be what is in Wayne's apartment. I won't even be here, just there.

It's pretty simple.

I always seem to know what I have to do next.

8

I mean, I had that place perfect, that Applebee's I was helping to open by the overpass. I wasn't a manager, just someone who really cared, a hard worker. The kitchen guys respected me because I was older than most of them. And the managers, I would hang out with them—bum cigarettes, shoot the shit, help them with their inventories anytime they asked. I stayed late, off the clock (district managers frown upon overtime), arranging the kitchen area, Windexing all the windows. I unloaded trucks and had the pantry stocked to the max, a clean organized library of canned and paper goods.

When I took the money opening night, right out of the cash register, I was thinking, "It's over." I was kind of happy, glad there was an end to all my hard work. I took the money so I could buy Jill a dress. Or maybe it was for a new alternator.

People were lined up outside to get in, business was booming, and one of the bartenders left the cash drawer behind the bar open. When he was in the back getting glasses, I took what I could. Just grabbed the bills, shoved them into my pockets, and ran out the back door, past the manager who thought I looked weird, I'm sure, past fellow Applebee's employees, out into the night.

I didn't have that much really, just a few hundred dollars, and I ran into the field behind the place. I don't know what I expected to see when I turned around. But it was just parked cars and the grill-smoke coming out of the restaurant's top vent.

The April night was chilly. I thought about what I had done. I was always on the verge of being a good guy—I had the smile, the look, the feelings, I was ready to be activated. But then something stopped me. My human-being card was always being spit out of the ATM.

I left, abandoning the restaurant I had helped to open, like a man abandoning his wife and newborn. I went to the liquor store and bought what I wanted: three bottles. I went back to my place and I crashed, and I drank a whole bottle in an hour. I puked and I drank some more.

9

This is the secret nobody ever tells you: there is so much happiness when you finally give in, a kind of happiness you can't imagine until you hit the very bottom. It's a magical pond you slip into headfirst, drowning quickly, though you take your time. There's quiet, and then there's not even quiet. It's just like that. And you're grateful.

Princess Is Sleeping

Carl is this older guy in church. He lost his wife a couple years ago to ovarian cancer. He stands about six foot, with a rugged but plain face and salt-and-pepper hair. He wears the same suit every Sunday, the same sweater and slacks on Wednesday nights. He never talks that much to other people in church, but somehow he pegged me as a kindred spirit.

Tonight, a Wednesday in March, I've gotten in early. The church has plush maroon carpeting and dark-wood pews, with three huge spaceship-looking chandeliers hovering overhead. I sit in a middle pew. Carl sits down next to me after a while. People stop by and say hello to us. Young couples, old couples, widowers, widows.

Michelle, Carl's mildly retarded daughter, sits on the other side of Carl. She looks a little messy in a green dress, with runs in her hose, but she seems to have pulled her outfit together the best she could. She is body-skinny, but her face is plump and round, like a flower with the petals pulled off.

"Dad?" she says.

"What, hon?" Carl looks over at her.

"Randy said we should buy pizza for all the people helping us move on Saturday."

"What's he going to do for money, Michelle?"

"I don't know."

Randy is Michelle's mildly retarded husband. They got married last year in a ceremony here. On Saturday, Michelle and Randy are moving into their new apartment, after living in a trailer Carl got them. Randy ruined it by trying to fix it up.

Randy comes striding in, in a suit that is a little too tight. He was born and raised in a poor section of town. Carl has taken him under his wing, helping Randy to be the best husband for his daughter. As a married couple, they make a pretty good living, considering. Michelle works at a big insurance office during the day, delivering all the inter-office mail. Randy works at Wendy's, doing maintenance.

"Hey, Carl!"

"Randy, bring it down a notch there," Carl says, looking around.

"Sorry."

As soon as Randy sits down beside Michelle, she beams out her worry-free glow.

"Michelle says you want to buy everybody pizza on Saturday. How you gonna do that, son?"

Randy smiles. He has stiff-looking, black hair he tries to tame with a wet comb. He looks over at me.

"Hey, Pete."

"Hey," I say. You have to like Randy. There's no way around it.

"You like pizza?"

"Yeah."

"Hey, Randy, I'm talking to you," Carl says.

The church is filling up. It's not as full as on Sunday nights, but there's a pretty big crowd.

"I'm sorry, Dad," Randy says.

"How you gonna pay for all the pizza?"

Randy grins. "You know me. I just see the big picture."

Carl laughs. You can tell, like everybody else in the church, he almost needs Randy to be Randy, like this.

"I'll donate the stupid money," Carl says, still laughing.

Tim Lewis and Karen his wife stop by the pew. Tim is going to be one of the guys to help move Michelle and Randy. He's a younger guy with reddish hair, skinny. His wife is a blonde bombshell. Tim reaches over and shakes Randy's hand.

"Hey, bud. You all ready for the big move? How's it going, Carl? Pete?"

Karen says, "Michelle, we're gonna throw you a big house-warming party once you guys get settled in."

Michelle just sits there beaming next to Randy, who stands up and says, "We're gonna buy you all pizza on move-day. Me and Dad worked it out."

Tim's eyes brighten, "That sounds good, bud."

Carl laughs. "Yup. He's got it all worked out, Tim."

Karen says, "I think I have somebody for you to meet, Pete. Her name's Jennifer, and she runs the front-desk at the workout place where I go…"

"Thanks, Karen. You got me a phone number?" I smile without making eye contact.

Karen takes a little card out of her purse. "Here you go. I told her you'd call."

"We better get us a seat," Tim says.

"We'll see you Saturday," Randy calls out as they walk away.

"Let's bring it down about two more notches," Carl whispers.

I look over at Carl. He is right next to me, and he smells like Old Spice and dryer-sheets.

"If she works at a gym," he whispers. "That's a good omen. Probably really good-looking."

"Yeah," I say.

"Dad," Randy yells, imitating a whisper.

"What?"

"How many pizzas you think we'll need?" He is very serious.

"Wait and see, okay?" Carl says, almost laughing but then again not.

The preacher comes up to the pulpit. We all stand up, like we're supposed to.

+

After the service, Carl and me drop off Randy and Michelle at their trailer. I leave my car at the church. Randy and Michelle don't want to go to Frisch's Big Boy with us because Randy is videotaping *Cops* and he's afraid his VCR won't come on.

The trailer is in a nice trailer park over by the only drive-in theater left in town. Theirs is the worst looking one though. Randy tried painting it this summer with some dark green house paint he got at Big Lots. He ran out and went back to the store, but they didn't have the same paint, so he wound up finishing with some light green. It's almost like he was trying to do camouflage. The funny thing is the trailer didn't need to be painted in the first place.

Michelle whispers bye, gets out, and then Randy crawls out from the backseat. Randy gestures for Carl to roll his window down. It's a nice night. The air smells real clean.

"So I'll call a bunch of pizza places and get prices," Randy says.

"You do that, son," Carl says.

Michelle goes on in, and then comes back out real quick.

"Randy! Where's Princess?"

Randy's eyes go into slits. Princess is the pet turtle Michelle found on the ground last fall over by the laundry facilities here. She thought it was a pretty rock, but it turned out to be a little store-bought turtle somebody had abandoned.

"She get out of her box?"

Michelle is stricken. "Yes!"

Randy looks in at Carl. "Don't worry, Dad. We'll find her. You go ahead and get something to eat."

"You sure?"

Sometimes Michelle can get so upset it turns into screaming and kicking. She's on nerve pills. Since Randy is a little more on the ball than she is, he's real good about reminding her to take them.

"I'll handle it, Dad."

"You sure?"

"Yeah, I got it."

Michelle is starting to cry, so Carl gets out of the car.

"I better help out."

I follow right behind. Inside, Michelle is pulling cushions off the couch and panting. Randy is trying to soothe her in a low-pitched country-singer voice: "Baby, it'll be okay. Princess is around here somewhere. I bet you anything she's asleep. Princess is sleeping, baby. Calm down."

Carl says, "Did you check under the dresser where she was last time?"

Michelle turns around, "Yes. Dad. I did. I checked there." She looks like she's ready to lose it.

I go into the kitchen. Randy has sort of messed it up by trying to build a plywood breakfast bar into the wall. I look under the dinette table, and there Princess is, by the heat register, her head stuck into her shell.

"I got you," I whisper, walking out and giving the turtle to Michelle. Carl and Randy are in the back bedroom scooting the dresser from the wall.

Michelle's joy is too big to fit the situation, of course, but still when she grabs hold of the thing and cuddles it. She looks innocent and caring, like life might be worth living after all.

"Thank you!" she says.

Carl and Randy come out into the living room. There's a big poster of Michael Jordan duct-taped to the wall, next to the one of Tim McGraw and Faith Hill. There's some good used furniture Randy hasn't ruined yet by trying to paint it or turn it into something else. Randy walks over to his wife.

"We're blessed," he says.

Carl looks a little roughed-up by all this.

"Michelle. Try to keep yourself calm. If you two want to live by yourselves and be normal, you can't be getting upset all the time."

"I know." She is still holding the turtle real tight.

Carl walks toward the door. I follow behind.

"We'll see you soon," Carl says.

"Bye, Dad! Bye, Pete!" Randy says. "I'll get some pizza prices and call you in the morning, Dad!"

+

After we have pie and coffee at the Frisch's, Carl and I drive on Princeton Road toward his condo. Carl's place is in a big complex, all ranch-styles with basements, brick with aluminum trim. In his little part of the yard he's got a small fountain.

We go in, past the work boots on the front porch. The only lights he turns on are in the hall. His wife decorated the place: eggshell-colored walls and a big mint-green sofa with lion-paw legs and light-colored carpet. There are landscape paintings and pretty lamps. As soon as he shuts the door, we go down the hall. We've been doing this for a while: Wednesday night church, pie and coffee, then this.

In his bedroom, we take off our clothes on separate sides of the bed, backs to each other, no lights on. The chain on the ceiling fan makes a little sound. I get in bed first, and he gets in right after. He kisses me. I like his warmth and I like the way he starts off tender and gets rough, moving me around to get at it.

We get dressed right after and go down to the basement he is in the middle of remodeling. Carl shows me where he wants to put in a ceiling light and a pool table.

"Yeah, I like playing pool," I say. "It's relaxing."

"It is, isn't it?"

The phone rings. Carl has to go upstairs. He hasn't had a phone line put in the basement yet. I can hear his voice.

"Hello? No, Randy. We'll order them the day of. Just forget about the pizzas, okay? How's Michelle? Good… Tell her to have a good night and that I love you both, okay? Yes. That's good."

I walk up to the kitchen. Carl is hanging up the phone.

"You want me to take you back to your car now?"

"Sure," I say.

+

The first time I knew about Carl was a month or so before Teresa, my wife, left me for another guy, almost a year ago now. Carl and me were out in the parking lot after church, just me and him. My car had a dead battery, and he had been nice enough to jump-start it. We stood out in the cold and snow as I ran my car to make sure nothing else was wrong with it.

White exhaust swirled around Carl's legs like he was some old sweet redneck lost at a rock concert. Teresa had had to work that night. Come to think of it, she was probably having her affair then. The lot had big hills of dirty snow plowed to its sides. The church lights were on.

"Thanks for helping out," I said.

Carl just smiled. But the smile had a feeling shining out of it, a need. He was so hungry and there were no words for his hunger, except everyday words sweetened by a look or a grip or a silence that took too long.

"Sure. Hey," he said, and he laughed.

I was hugging myself against the cold, thinking of his cracked-leather skin and of the veins at the top of his hands that had throbbed when he put the jumper-cable clamps on the batteries, me just standing there watching while he did everything. That's the way he did stuff.

"What?" I said.

He came up closer.

"You like coconut cream pie?"

I smiled back, and I said yes. My heart got big. I imagined my heart was some exotic plant that could grow in a dark place overnight.

+

At home, my stomach hurts a little. I watch TV and then take a shower. I watch more TV and eat some Fat Free Pringles. My house has been up for sale since two days after Teresa left me for that guy she met at work named Glenn. Tomorrow afternoon, the realty lady said she would be bringing a married couple over. I imagine them walking through while I'm not here. What they'll see is pretty nice. Teresa did a good job choosing the furniture and all.

I get the business card out of my jacket pocket and call that gal Karen told me about. It's almost 11:00, and I'm worried about waking her up.

"Hello?"

"Hey. Is this Jennifer?"

"Yeah."

"I hope I didn't wake you up."

"Who is this?"

"I'm Pete Wells. Karen Lewis gave me your number. She said she talked to you about me, and I don't normally do this kind of stuff…"

"I'm sorry but I was almost asleep. Why don't you call me tomorrow afternoon? I am just wiped out."

"Sorry."

"That's okay."

"I'll call you later."

I put the card back in my wallet, knowing it will disappear anyway. It will melt like a snowflake on a windshield. At least I tried.

+

Friday, at 2:00 in the afternoon—generally a dead period in the video-rental biz—I am inventorying the candy on the shelves under the register when an FTD delivery guy sets a bouquet of flowers on the counter. Angie, the clerk who's on with me, asks the guy who it's for.

Princess Is Sleeping

"Pete Wells."

I go over and sign.

"Aren't you lucky?" Angie says, batting her lashes. She's an overweight divorcee who is always kidding around.

I nod and smile, trying not to make a big deal. I'm the manager here, so I'm all the time putting up with smart-alecky attitudes. This is the first time anybody has ever sent me flowers in my whole entire life though. Pink carnations and white roses and gladiolas in a professional display. I think they are from Carl. I plot out how I won't read the card to Angie.

Here's what it says: "I miss you and I want your forgiveness… Your loving wife, Teresa."

"Who sent them?" Angie says.

"My loving wife."

"That bitch?"

"Yeah."

Angie laughs, running a returned video under the scanner. I smile at her and get choked up but not really that much. I never want to be disappointed by real life.

"She wants my forgiveness," I say.

Angie laughs again.

"It's gonna take more than flowers," she says, like she could even know.

I just nod my head.

+

Teresa calls me at the house that night. I'm eating a Healthy Start beef-tips dinner, the flowers in front of me on the table.

Teresa says, "I *thought* you might like flowers."

"They're beautiful."

"I want to talk. Can we meet somewhere and talk?"

"About what?"

She doesn't say anything. I keep looking at the flowers.

"I think the house might have sold today. The realty lady brought a couple through and she left me a message…"

"She left me one too. That's what made me send you the flowers. Glenn left last week. He got a job in Michigan and he's gone and it's just, it's just, I'm miserable, Pete. I feel like crap… Can we meet somewhere?"

"Yeah, sure."

"How about Olive Garden in a half hour, over by the mall?"

"Sure."

So we meet up there and she drinks red wine and I drink Diet Coke. She eats, but I don't because I had the Healthy Start. She looks skinny in jeans and a pink blouse. She's done something to the color of her brown hair. It looks redder.

"I can't take it. I can't, Pete. I miss you."

"Hey, I miss you too."

Automatically, in my head, I start going over all the reasons I love Teresa: the way she fixes up things, her cooking, her attention to detail. I like the way, when she gets tired, her voice goes raspy. I like the way she gulps her red wine.

"I'm a mess with you, but an even bigger one without you," she says. "I don't care if we have sex or not. I don't need sex. I don't. I've figured that out. *We* don't need it."

I smile. For the last year or so of our marriage I couldn't fake the sex-part any more. I mean, I tried sometimes. We even did bubble baths and stuff.

"We can try again," I say.

"You always just tell me what I want to hear," she says. She looks at me like she's both mad and grateful, and grateful has finally won out.

"That's why I love you," she says. She picks up the napkin off her lap and wipes her eyes. I notice she's got some sauce on her blouse, just a little bit.

Teresa leaves her car in the Olive Garden parking lot because I am afraid she is too drunk to drive. I feel chivalrous and in charge. I drive her to our house.

In our kitchen, smelling the flowers, she says, "These puppies are prettier than what I thought. I ordered them off the internet."

"They're beautiful," I say.

She comes over and kisses me.

You have to close off certain portions of yourself, like a house with rooms you don't want to heat. In our bedroom, she gets naked and I get naked and I have missed her that way you miss people you are supposed to miss. I am able to do it, like her taking off with Glenn was just the vacation I needed. I kiss her very deeply. She lies under me and I think about Carl and the way he moves it into me, the way his face looks sunburned as he pushes himself up inside me. She bites her lips real soft and I think about how every single thing human beings do is a big act, like everybody is in a big-budget serious movie and everybody is guessing what the director wants. I see Teresa as

Sandra Bullock and me as Keanu Reeves. For a second or two, things are the way they are supposed to be.

After we're done, Teresa laughs lovingly.

"Why, you did miss me, didn't you?"

"Yes, I did. I most certainly did."

+

The next morning, we drive over to Michelle and Randy's new apartment. Outside is a big U-Haul truck, and eight guys from the church are already unloading it. Ken is carrying in a couple pulled-out dresser drawers. I park at the next building over because there's no room near the new apartment. Teresa and I walk over to where all the action is.

Randy is in a pair of sweatpants and a Kenny Chesney concert tee-shirt. He has the expression on his face of a cop directing traffic, standing out there in the sun with his big plastic mug of coffee, the kind they give you at the convenience store for ninety-nine-cent refills.

"Hey, Pete! Hey, Teresa! I didn't know you guys were back together!" He laughs loudly and out of real joy.

Tim stops and looks over and smiles, like he knew things would just have to end up this way. I have to admit I like the feeling of being seen as a couple all over again.

"Where's Carl?" I ask.

"Inside. Ain't it the perfect day to be moving?" Randy says.

Teresa looks a little put off, like now that we're back together she's dreading being part of the church again. She's more of a loner than I am.

Inside the apartment, Carl and Michelle are putting a sheet on the mattress in the bedroom. Carl looks up from putting the fitted end over a corner. He's in his gray overalls. When he sees Teresa and me, something registers on his face for about a half second, a glint in his eyes like a flash of sun on a wristwatch.

Michelle looks up. "Princess is in her box in the bathroom," she whispers, for no reason.

"That's good," I say.

"She's in there. I put her in there," Michelle says. "She is safe."

Carl says, "Hey, Teresa. Good seeing you." He smiles great big, and comes over and hugs her.

We can still do it if you want, I want to tell Carl. In fact, Teresa coming back is better for everyone involved. She knows that I like guys. Not that we talk about it, but she knows from the magazines I've had and thrown away, and from that one time I got into phone-sex for about a month. Every time she caught me, she just gave me the evil eye. One time, she put a Post-It note on the dirty magazine she found. It said, "I feel sorry for you."

"I'm glad you guys are working it out," Carl says. He looks over at me, grinning. "This one here. He's been a mess without you."

Michelle goes and gets Princess. Her head is inside her shell. There's a half-bit strawberry in her box and a faded orange washcloth.

"*Shhhhhh,*" Michelle whispers. "She's sleeping."

Carl laughs. "Well, put her back in the bathroom and shut the door, dumb-dumb."

Carl and me and Teresa go out and start bringing more stuff in.

A half hour later, two Domino's Pizza cars pull up beside the U-Haul. Randy directs the two delivery guys (one great big and the other one short and skinny) toward us. The backseats of both cars are filled up almost to the roofs with pizza boxes.

"This way, boys," Randy yells.

Carl comes out the front door right about then and suddenly looks shocked. "What is going on?"

Randy comes up. "I went ahead and called, Dad."

"You *what?*"

"I ordered thirty, Dad," Randy says, down to business, all smiles. He is like that. He doesn't listen once he is onto something. "I figured people would be coming and going all day and might get hungry."

"I told you the both of us would call!" Carl yells.

Everybody freezes. Carl is being way too loud.

"Yeah, but you were busy," Randy says. He doesn't even know that there are only about ten people here total, and that nobody else is going to show up. Thirty pizzas for ten people is just plain reckless. But Randy does not get that, even right now with Carl looking like he might explode.

"I told you, goddammit!" Carl says.

I walk toward them. Teresa is inside the house still, helping Michelle arrange her kitchen. As I move toward the two of them, Randy's face goes blank and then he gets a little tight-eyed.

"Dad, you're cussing."

Carl steps closer to Randy. The guys from the church are behind me.

Carl says, "You are goddamned right I'm cussing, you little dumb-ass!"

The pizza guys just stand there, caught in the crossfire. I go over to Carl and get real close.

"Hey, Carl," I say. "Calm down, now. We can work this out." My voice is like the voice Carl uses when he talks to his mildly retarded daughter.

Randy says, "You're cussing, Dad. You tell *me* cussing is wrong, Dad. That's what you say." Randy imitates Carl's low-pitched serious way of talking, "*Now, son, cussing is wrong.*"

Carl looks at me. He has tears in his eyes. He looks so helpless and so lost, I want him to kiss me. I want him to come back to life that way. When he punches me in the face, I see the trees and the sky blur into melted glass. The whole world sharpens into one little bloody point, like a needle prick. It's my nose he broke. I hit the ground like I've fallen off a roof in a cartoon.

Tim and another guy from church pull Carl away from me. He is already apologizing and crying. I don't think people have ever seen Carl cry before. It'll be a story for a while, but then nothing.

I sit up, blood pouring down my top lip. Teresa and Michelle come out of the apartment.

Teresa yells right off, "What in the hell?"

Randy is beside me, saying in his loudest voice, "Oh my gosh, Dad. Dad! You don't hit people, Dad. Not in the face. That could cause permanent damage! Oh my gosh, Dad!"

Carl stands there like he has finally found out there is an end to something he never even knew the beginning of. All of a sudden, my mind flashes on me and Carl doing it. How I feel all melted and beautiful, how I even moan real loud. I mean, I am still me: five foot ten and skinny and a little pale, anonymous in the face with brown hair and brown eyes. But I am someone else too. Someone somebody catches and holds down and loves.

I stand up. Teresa is holding me on one side. Carl goes over by the U-Haul truck, rubbing his head, with Tim and a couple other guys. He is looking down at the ground. The two pizza guys stand there like this whole thing is their fault. But still, you can tell, they want to get paid.

KEITH BANNER lives in Cincinnati, Ohio. He has published two works of fiction, *The Life I Lead*, a novel, and *The Smallest People Alive*, a book of stories, as well as numerous short stories and essays in magazines and journals, including *American Folk Art Messenger, Other Voices, Washington Square, Kenyon Review*, and *Third Coast*. He received an O. Henry Prize for his short story "The Smallest People Alive," and an Ohio Arts Council individual artist fellowship for fiction. *The Smallest People Alive* was named one of the best books of 2004 by *Publishers Weekly*. He is also the co-founder of Visionaries + Voices, a studio for artists with disabilities, and Thunder-Sky, Inc., an outsider art gallery.

CPSIA information can be obtained at www.ICGtesting.com
Printed in the USA
BVOW03s2022170315

392123BV00002B/18/P